The
Fairy
⟨∞ of ∞⟩
London Town

VOLUME TWO
See-Saw Sacradown

SHREWSBURY HOUSE SCHOOL

ALTA PETO

PLUS PRIZE

Freddie Windsor

~ November 1999 ~

Other titles by William Mayne published by
Hodder Children's Books

Earthfasts

Cradlefasts

The Fairy Tales of London Town
Volume One: Upon Paul's Steeple

The Fox Gate

The Fairy Tales

of

London Town

VOLUME TWO
See-Saw Sacradown

William Mayne

*Hodder
Children's
Books*

A division of Hodder Headline plc

Published by Hodder Children's Books 1996

This edition published by Hodder Children's Books 1997

10 9 8 7 6 5 4 3 2 1

ISBN 0340 64861 9

Printed and bound in Great Britain

Hodder Children's Books
A Division of Hodder Headline plc
338 Euston Road
London NW1 3BH

For Josse Emanuel

⮴ Contents ⮴

∽ *See-Saw, Sacradown* ∽

See-saw, Sacradown
  Which is the way to London Town?
One foot up, and one foot down,
  That is the way to London Town.

———————

∽ *The Lime Kill* ∽

Years ago there were lime kills, but in case you do not
know what they are, I will tell you. They are the
ovens where lime rock is baked to powder to spread
on the farmland to make the soil sweet. They are built out
of stone, and the fire goes in at one side and stone in at the
top.

Well, that is that. But one of the lime kills that baked lime
for the King of London was used for another purpose. A
witch from Chippenham had caught a young Welsh prince,
Cradock, and imprisoned him in it so that he could not get
out. All his food was brought by toads, who were prisoners
themselves. The witch was either dead or gone a long time
to Devizes market, or forgetful with ale in a ditch round
Malmesbury somewhere. The lime kill had trees growing
all round it now.

Now, the King of London's daughter just about had to
work like anyone's daughter, on her father's farm. There
was a big lot of farms at London then. There must have
been for this story to come about.

This girl was named Demelza, and she worked away as
usual in the fields, until the rain came, and she went to
shelter in a little wood. And then it was night and she stayed
where she was, and then it was day, and she did not know

which way to get back to the field, and so it was for nine nights, and she could not get herself out of the wood. You see, this was because of the spell that was on the place. You will find out if you listen.

Demelza found a little hut made of stone. She knew it was a lime kill, and put her back against it and waited to die, being nine days hungry and nine nights lost.

But she was not far into dying when Cradock inside the kill called out and asked, "Who are you? Where do you come from? Where do you want to go?" It was Cradock, wondering whether the witch had come back, calling louder and louder because his voice was lost in the mortar between the stones.

"Who am I? I am Demelza," she said. "I come from my father's castle and I am lost. He is the King of London. I wish to go home to him, and I am so hungry."

"You are enchanted by the magic of the witch who put me here," said Cradock. "It spreads all round. But I can help you to find your way home again. Listen. I am a prince, just as you are a princess."

Well, she listened to his voice coming little out from the wall, without quite understanding how a lime kill could speak and be a prince. But in those days girls accepted what they were told, and perhaps she was younger than you think.

"I will help you find your way home again," said Cradock. "But you will have to promise to do what I say."

"Anything," said Demelza. And she meant it, so hungry and cold and lost. But of course she wondered what she could do for a lime kill.

"If you are to marry me," said Cradock, "you must bring

a knife and cut through the wall."

"I will," she said. But she knew she could never find her way there again.

Then the toads that looked after Cradock brought her forest bread, which is acorns, and led her to the edge of the field. Now the harvest was over, and the fields empty, but she found her way to her father's castle.

He was pleased to see her after all those days. "But something is troubling you," he said. "What is, Demelza? If there is something in my country of London that will set you right, then you shall have it."

"I need a knife," said Demelza. "That will take my trouble away."

"But do not speak like that," said the King.

"But what else can I do?" asked Demelza. "I was lost, and then a lime kill found me, and I promised to take a knife to it and cut out one of its stones and then to marry it. It is a prince, it says."

"It is a royal lime kill," said the King. "But no prince."

"Well, I have promised," said Demelza.

"Now then," said the King, "you are a princess. You need not go yourself. We shall send another girl. How would a lime kill know the difference?"

So they did that, and called for the miller's daughter to go in Demelza's place.

"He will be pleased with her," said the King. "She is as pretty as a sack of wheat."

So far so good. The miller's daughter went out to the field and into the wood, and she found the lime kill. She did as she was told and began to dig out one of the stones.

It took her all day and all night, and the stone was as firmly fixed as ever.

Then Cradock inside said, "I hear the sun rise."

"It is risen," said the miller's daughter. "If I could not see it I would hear the shutters of my father's mill sails being opened and closed."

"Then you must go at once and help him," said Cradock. "And send the king's daughter to me."

His voice was quiet, but in his anger it was fierce. The miller's daughter took the knife and ran all the way to the castle, to tell the King what had happened.

"Then we must try again," said the King. "I am not to be ordered about by a lime kill."

But he and Demelza tried another turn. They sent for the pig-keeper's daughter, who was pretty as a pig, and sent her to the lime kill instead.

So she scraped away a day and a night, and at daybreak Cradock said, "I hear the sun waking."

"That's so," said the pig-keeper's daughter. "I hear my father calling 'Pig-how, pig-how,' so that they come one and all to the trough."

"Then you go one and all and sharpish to the King and tell him his daughter must come here this day, and that if she does not, then his castle and his kingdom of London will fall to ruin, and for yourself the pigs will die, and for the miller the stones will break, and it will be the end."

"Yes, master," said the pig-keeper's daughter, and ran off at once and blubbed out her story to the King.

And when she heard it the princess Demelza was ashamed of what she had done, took the knife warm from the girl's hand, and hurried to the lime kill.

"I am sorry," she said. "I am sorry."

But inside the lime kill the prince was too proud to speak, and let Demelza work away.

She worked for two hours, and whether it was true love or fear we do not know, but at the end of that time she pulled out a stone on to her lap, and set it aside.

Then she looked in, and understood at last that the lime kill did not speak, but that the voice came from a good-looking young prince, dressed in cloth of gold, decorated with jewels, and shining with them. She fell straight in love with him, and was so pretty herself, looking in confused and blushing with shame at what she had done, and realising how filled with mortification she would have been if the miller's daughter or the pig-keeper's daughter had won this young man – that he fell truly in love with her too. Well now, being a princess warrants nothing; you can be fat or thin, vile or bonny.

She then dug him out, and he dug out to her, and he came out.

"You are to be mine," he said. "I am to be yours. Let us leave now for Wales and say nothing to any person but fly at once."

"But," said Demelza, "I should tell my father the King of London, or he will sorrow again."

"Well then, away," said Cradock. "But do not say more than three words to him and come away at once."

It can't all be said in three words, and it wasn't. When Demelza came back to the lime kill it had fallen completely into ruin, as if it had never been. And the prince was no longer there.

"But now I have something to love," said Demelza. "And I shall do so."

She went back to the castle to say farewell, and then returned to the wood and the lime kill. For nine days and nights she waited, hoping that the prince would return to that place. But he did not.

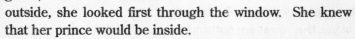

So on the ninth night she crossed to the far side of the wood, to go further. And from there she saw a light and thought it was a house.

When she came to it in the grass, with its firewood outside, she looked first through the window. She knew that her prince would be inside.

She saw a table spread with gold dishes and silver goblets, and smelt the food and wine. But there was no prince, only toads, large and small.

"He is hiding," she thought, and knocked at the door. But only a little toad came to let her in; and the other toads made her welcome.

"How did you come? What do you want?" they asked.

"I wish to have spoken three words only," said Demelza, telling her story all through. We have heard it and already remember.

"Well then," said the greatest toad, and he brought out from the wall a chest and opened it, and they gave her three thatching needles, a millstone, and three pig nuts, and then they sent her on her way.

So she went on it, with the needles and the great stone, and the three little nuts.

"Of what use are they?" she wondered. "I would go home, but I love him so."

Then she came to a mountain of ice, with the sky at the top, and had to go up it or go home. She used the thatching needles to make steps, driving one in and standing on it, driving in the second and standing on that and holding the third and lifting out the lowest one; and oh, the weariness of dragging up the millstone to the sky.

But at last she had done it, and was ready to go down the other side.

But here there were swords standing in the way, too close to walk among, too sharp to lay aside.

But she rode upon the millstone and broke her way through, and thought her troubles were done, and she had not yet had to eat a pig nut.

She came to a castle and, well, yes, it was grander than her father's castle at London, so she was too shy to go in as herself, but not too proud to look for a place as a servant.

And she thought she saw the prince Cradock on the wall and looking down, golden and bright. And if it was not him, why he would do just as well.

So at a side door she was taken on as a kitchen-maid, because there was much work on hand at that time.

Why? It is better not to ask, but the truth is, the princess Eunice at that castle was to be married, and who was she to take as husband but Cradock the beautiful; and he, after this long time, thought that Demelza had not wanted him, because she had not come back.

Demelza was not given food to prepare, but set to scouring pots. This work grew heavier and heavier upon her as she heard what feast she was helping to prepare. And if salt will scour pots, then tears will do it better, and those pots be the cleanest yet.

So at the end of the day she was miserable and hungry, and took from her pocket a pig nut, to eat that and make her meal of it.

But when she rubbed the skin to take it off the whole nut unfolded in her hand, and unwrapped itself and became a dress like a wedding gown.

The other servants saw the dress, and sent for the princess Eunice, and Eunice begged for the dress to wear at her wedding.

"It is too good for me," said Demelza. "I will let you have it and willingly, but let me have the honour of sleeping outside the door of the prince."

"That I will do," said Eunice, taking up the pretty dress. But at the same time she said to herself, "I do not trust that handsome kitchen-maid," and she put a sleep powder into Cradock's wine.

So it was in vain that Demelza lay outside, while she told him through the keyhole how she had freed him in the wild wood from the lime kill. He did not hear.

So she went back to her work in the scullery, dressing the birds for the feast. And at the end of the day she could not bear to eat more than a pig nut.

But the pig nut uncurled in her hands and out came a

radiant dress that almost stood by itself, so rich was its embroidery and so thick its petticoats.

"But this I must have again," said Eunice.

"I will sleep again across the prince's threshold," said Demelza. "That is all the price."

"That I will pay," said Eunice. But she said to herself, "This is a scheming piece," and put the powder in the glass again.

And once again, no matter how she wailed and called and told Cradock of the house of toads in the wood, he heard nothing.

But a great number of folk in the castle heard what she had to say, and told Prince Cradock, to make him laugh. And he wondered, and he wondered. But he could not send for a kitchen-maid, since this was not his own castle. "I shall do nothing," he said. "I am used to it after those years in the lime kill."

Nothing is a short way of saying it. Not to drink the wine at night is nothing, and that is what he did. Not a drop of it passed his lips, but all of it was taken by Eunice.

Before that, you know the way the tales go, Demelza had taken the third pig nut, and between her fingers it became a golden wedding dress. And once again Eunice said she must have it, and once again Demelza lay across the prince's threshold.

"Nothing will come it," said Eunice.

Once more Demelza wept at her misfortune, and this time Cradock heard her through the keyhole. He had spent years listening through cracks in the lime kill and heard her well.

"I freed you from the lime kill, I visited the house of toads, I climbed the ice mountain, and I came through the standing swords," Demelza said.

All at once the door opened for her, and Cradock was there, saying, "It is truth. I have waited for you until you never came. But now you are here you shall stay with me for ever."

And then, midnight as it was, and Eunice being asleep with the wine, they rolled across the swords, climbed the ice mountain, and went to the feast at the house of toads.

The toads were enchanted by that same Chippenham witch, and now they were freed. And the little house turned into a fine castle with a moat, which was home for the toads, who ran about in joy.

And from there they sent for the King of London, who was glad to come to Cradock, who was now the King of Wales. And between them they ruled London and all England and all Wales too.

∽ *Down the Well* ∽

One moonlit night a hungry town fox was prowling about behind B——— P———, where he met a little kitten belonging to You-know-who, God bless her.

"You're not much of a meal for a starving creature," said the fox. "But in these hard times something is always better than nothing."

"Put me down a minute," said the kitten. "I live here, and I belong to You-know-who, and I know where the cheeses are stored. Follow me and you'll see."

You have to live by your wits in these places.

She led him into the yard at the back, where Somebody kept Her Horses, and here there was a deep well with two buckets for watering them, one up at the top, one down at the bottom. "Now, look in here," she said, "and you will see the big cheese," she said.

"Her, you mean?" asked the fox. "I'm not fit to be seen, only dressed in my working clothes."

"Don't trouble about that," said the kitten, who hadn't got that night's nightly saucer of full-cream milk from A Certain Person. "Right away down there at the bottom."

The fox peered down the well, and saw the moon reflected in the water. "It looks like Her on a new sixpence," he said. "Is my hair tidy?"

"Oh, grow up," said the kitten, who would rather have been a cougar belonging to an indulgent president. But we all have day-dreams. "If you want something to eat this is the way."

She jumped into the top bucket. There were two, you know, one to go up and the other to go down, and then change places. But in a democracy you are always pulling up the full ones.

Round and round the windlass went, and down went the kitten towards the water. She had been down before, some trick of Someone's great grand-children, so she knew what to do, which is, climb out of the bucket, before it goes into the water, and cling on to the rope, because before long it is pulled up. So she did that, way down far.

"Bring up the cheese, like you said," said the fox. "This bucket only has water in it." Because that's how they come up a well, remember.

"It's too heavy for me to lift alone," said the kitten. "You'd best must come down. Don't make a noise. She's got a gun, you know, and twenty dogs, and every soldier."

You must live by your wits in these places.

The fox tipped the water out of the bucket. The kitten got wet, but that was better than being swallowed. The fox climbed into the bucket, and before he even got comfortable it began to whizz down the well, deeper and deeper.

And the kitten went whirring up like nobody's business (but it was Somebody's house), shot out of the well like a rocket, and landed on Somebody's lap, who was sitting in bed reading about horses.

She got thrown out because she was soaking wet.

The fox spent a long time trying to get the cheese into the bucket and complaining about the matter. There was no one to help him.

In the morning You-know-who complained she could not drink her tea because it had such a funny taste, and the horses were very uptight about their breakfast drink too. The fox had stopped complaining. Perhaps he was not feeling well.

In these places you can only live by the wits you have, if they last long enough.

∽ *The Three-legged Dog* ∽

The three-legged dog
  At Waterloo
Sniffed his own tail
  And said "How do ye do?"

∽ *Riding to Market* ∽

T here was a man at Ealing who was going to sell the
family donkey in the market at Epping, where there
was a good trade in them for the charcoal burners
in the forest. The man and his boy set off with the donkey
early in the day.

At first the father rode on the donkey, and so they got
along. But at Acton they met a social worker, who wrote
stuff down and made some comments about how fathers
should have a thought for their children and not sit on a
donkey while the poor little lad ran alongside. "I've a good
mind to carry out my duty and report you," he said. "The
boy should be in council care."

It's all very well not taking any notice, but they can fit you up. So the man said, "It's the boy's turn to Kensington," and got off.

"I shall still report the matter," said the social worker, and the donkey said, "Hee-haw."

So now the son rode and the man led, and they went on their way.

But somewhere by White City they met a schoolmaster strutting out for an airing. He tapped the boy on his shoulder with his walking stick, and brushed up a moustache.

"Courtesy and consideration," he said, "are what I teach my pupils. Get off your donkey, sir, and let that poor old man ride on it. I shall see the matter is put on your curriculum report. You should be ashamed of yourself."

So the boy got off, the schoolmaster tickled him with the stick, and marched away, left, right, tap.

"God save the scholars," said the father, "we had best all walk, you on two, me on two, and the ass on four. However it is, eight legs are quicker than three."

They went on, and somewhere about Marble Arch they met townsfolk who did never a thing for themselves except swallow.

"Look at these poor vagrants," they said. "Not the sense between them to sit on the creature. Why walk when you can ride? Such fools not to."

"Well, that does seem the way," said the father. "I didn't think of it, indeed. I'll get up and you can pillion behind, and that's sense."

So the pair of them rode, and the little donkey went along Holborn Road, through the City as if he knew it, and into

Whitechapel Road; and if he wasn't racing, well, he wasn't going backwards.

But in Mile End Road a fellow in uniform put up his hand and stopped them.

"Royal Society for the Prevention of," he said. "Local Inspector. This matter has been reported. How is it that a well-grown lad cannot walk, and that a full-grown man rides with him on a donkey just a quarter the weight of all three of them?"

"I'm not into the mathematics," said the man. "But it's a very strong ass, or it wouldn't do it."

"It has to do what it is told," said the man in uniform. "Or no doubt it is whipped."

"I see you know about asses," said the man.

The Inspector was writing down by now.

"It'll be a warning this time," he said. "Next time the donkey goes to a retirement home, and you to the lock-up."

He snapped his notebook shut, opened it again for another note, and strode off to a worse case, where a lady had been swearing at a parrot.

"Well now," said the man with the donkey, "we can't all three walk, and yet we've tried everything, so what's with it?

You've been latest in school, so you tell me what you've learned."

"Just up ahead," said the boy, "is Mile End Station on the Metropolitan Line, and at the end of the line is Epping."

"Well, you should have said so at the beginning," said his father. "It is Metropolitan Line all the way from Ealing and we could have ridden the whole way and if there wasn't a chair the donkey would hold us."

So they got themselves tickets and settled to ride on the Underground. That went well, but in a while the other passengers began to say it wasn't a cattle truck, though most days they complained and said it was.

They called the ticket collector, and he took the man's ticket, and the boy's, and the donkey's, and told them they got off here, if you please. "Here are the Rules," he said, bringing out his book in black print. "And here are the Regulations," and they were in red.

"We won't argue," said the man.

"You won't," said the ticket collector. "Be on your way."

And on their way they went, put off the train at Loughton. When they were at the road again they wondered how to get along, since two riding would not do, and neither of them suited alone, or not at all.

And the donkey was thinking that all this was enough, and not lifting his feet off the pavement.

"There's just the one thing for it," said the lad, after a bit. "It isn't the biggest donkey in the world, for all it's so strong."

And he hunted about until he found a wooden joist from some demolition, and a length of blind-cord from the front room of the same place.

"I see what you are at," said the man, when the boy brought these things back.

Between them they tied the donkey's feet together, and then strung it on the joist, and carried it like that into Epping.

This made the donkey sing, so that when they came into the market not only the charcoal burners were roaring louder than the donkey at them, but all the people at the market were falling about with laughter. They never saw a donkey brought in like that by two foolish people from Ealing, or anywhere.

And a man from the Council came and told them that they needed a licence for entertaining in public, so show it, or buy one.

"Now," said the man, "it's clear we can never please everyone, and maybe we shouldn't listen to any of them, only to ourselves."

And he and his son decided that no donkey could be happy at Epping, whereas they were all content at Ealing.

So they walked back, no richer, but wiser. At Epping they have forgotten what they are laughing at and sound like asses themselves.

∽ *In Lambeth Marsh* ∾

About ninety years ago, when Bishop Robert was a boy, he was nearly lost for ever. It was not his fault. No one knows whose fault it was, except that very person. And he won't say, and we don't know his name.

One October day Robert was with his parents, his brother, and his sister waiting at Leicester Square Underground Station for a train to Totteridge and Whetstone (which are just one place) and tea.

And something came along the tracks that was not a train. It was never clear who it was. Robert later always thought of him as Lambo.

Lambo came shuffling and hopping along, in his great white skin and the gingery long fur that is not quite hair and is not quite feathers, but something in between: if you get near, look, and you will see the hairs have branches.

He came along on his marshy feet, exploring the tunnel. He was upright and huge. He had flaps over his nostrils to keep out water, so he breathed snortingly. Some people at Baker Street thought he was a lost steam engine on the wrong line.

He smelt of bubbly, muddy, greenish marsh or swamp. It is how he is. After all, man smells worst of anything to most other animals.

The people on the platform stopped their talk. "Typical," was all they said. "But we are probably to blame for living on the Northern Line."

Then they were quiet and watched Lambo going on his way. He did not look at them. Perhaps he did not like their smell.

Flop, flop, went his feet. The people on the platform kept quite still and wished their train would come and take them all straight home. They all wanted their teas too. They did not think what Lambo might want – sometimes it is better not to.

Next to Robert stood a naughty boy, the very person whose name we do not know, who will not say. This boy had in his pocket a conker, which he was keeping for some big fight. Or for something worse.

Now was the time for something worse, something not very wise.

The boy took the conker from his pocket, breathed on it, polished it a last time, tightened his lip, bent his elbow, took good aim, and threw it at Lambo. It hit Lambo on the side of the head.

Lambo stopped his walk, and turned, and looked. Two hundred faces looked full at him. Four hundred eyes had already been looking secretly.

Lambo put out a long and hairy/feathery arm. He picked up Robert, tucked him under the long and hairy/feathery arm, and walked on into the tunnel with him. Both disappeared into the darkness. Lambo did not say a word.

Robert was very interested in what was happening, but somehow did not have enough breath to say so. On the platform his father and mother, his brother and his sister, had leapt forward with a shout and cry. But they were too late, because at once a train drew in, ran the length of the platform, and blocked the entrance to the tunnel.

Robert's father said to the driver, "Stop."

The driver said, "I have, mate, or you wouldn't be stood there talking to me. You'd be running at forty miles an hour."

"Don't go any further," said Robert's father. "There's a monster, an alien, on the track."

"Time you went home and took it easy, mate," said the driver. "Get in if you're getting in. There's my green light, and off I go."

Robert's mother wasted no time on words. She got into the train and pulled the alarm, and the train could not go. She did not want it to run over the greenish monster, because the greenish monster was carrying her son Robert. This was very thoughtful of her, because she had no idea he would one day be a bishop.

But now, today, there was confusion, and tumult, and policemen of several kinds running in to sort the matter out. So it was some time before anyone got the story straight, even longer before it was believed, and quite dark outside as well as in before anyone got into the tunnel and followed after Lambo and his captive.

There was nothing to be found, nothing to be seen. Somewhere under the London streets Lambo had got away.

"Underground Tragedy," the *Standard* said that night. "Monster Steals Helpless Boy."

"Probable Kidnap," said the *Telegraph* in the morning.

"Grisly Horror at Leicester Square," said the *Sketch*, and people queued all day at the cinema to see such a film.

We must leave them for the time being, abandon the anguished parents, two hungry siblings, a baffled police force, and an angry station-master. We shall have to look at Lambo's history. We shall not find out who actually threw the conker.

But you can see the conker tree still, growing just behind the Bishop's Palace, where Robert has often seen it but does not know there is a coincidence.

Long before men came to the Thames and grunted about, hunting elephants where London now stands, there was a fine patch of swamp. The Thames went down the middle, and the marshes stretched along either side. In the muddy places, among the wild birds, on the south side, Lambo had his home.

Someone knew about him once, because the marshy place was called Lambeth, after him. Or perhaps he was called Lambo after Lambeth.

Certainly he was a monster, but monsters are allowed. He had his family in the marshes, and they were all monsters too. He loved them monstrously. They live a long time, and they take hundreds of years to grow, but they do not worry, because there are no monster schools.

When ships came up the river Lambo swam to them and winked at the figureheads, but those lovely ladies only smiled and said nothing. Mrs Lambo said, "Don't talk to them, Lambo dear, we don't know who they are."

So Lambo did not swim that way again. He ignored the sailors and lounged about the swamp, still happy.

One day, though, he swam up the river and saw a curious thing. There was a bridge, and on the bridge a horse and cart.

"I will not have you talking to the cart," said Mrs Lambo. "It has disgraceful wheels. And neither of us believes in horses, I hope."

"Indeed no," said Lambo. "Quite imaginary."

But men were coming, and horses, and carts, and cows. And more ships came. Lambo began to find curious things in the marsh, spoiling the texture and flavour of the mud.

Boys came to the water's edge and dangled hooks for fish. Lambo could catch fish easy. Sometimes he would hang one on a hook; sometimes he would hang a boot; and often eat the bait-worm or tasty maggot.

But as time went by, and before the children were many monster years older, men had built walls round the marsh, and started to dry it up. They built houses at the edge. They built a palace for a bishop. Lambo never heard about bishops. He thought the first house he saw was a stranded ship, and helpfully pushed it back into the river. He was very much shouted at.

"Do not help them any more, Lambo," said his wife. "We do not want them helping us. I wonder what sort of thing they are?"

"We could try one for supper," said Lambo.

"They do not look very wholesome," said his wife. "There are maggots, and there are maggots."

At last there were railways round the marsh; there were factories at the edge; there were roads across it; there were lights on long poles. There was a tiresome ferry boat that went through their bedroom twenty times a day. At length there was not enough marsh to live in.

"We could try the Zoo," said Lambo.

"It costs two pounds to get in," said Mrs Lambo. "We don't have money."

Actually they had quite a lot of money that Lambo had found here and there. The children kept it in a box, thinking the coins were immature buttons that had not yet developed holes.

Lambo, looking for a safe place to live, found some lovely drains. There was not much view, but the mud was good. That was how Lambo became an underground creature, exploring in tunnels and seeing where they went.

There are more tunnels than you hear about, under London. Lambo knew them all. If he can't get up there himself he puts along his hairy/feathery arm, and then a fine, feeling finger. Look in the gullies along the street and see him move his wrist.

"A Tube tunnel is not the best," he said. "Good and roomy, but far too dry. I use them for a short cut now and then. I have to look out for worms, though." He meant the trains. "But there's a lovely tingly wire on the floor." He meant the live rail.

"Don't get talking to worms," said Mrs Lambo. She stayed with the children in an outfall by the docks.

This is where we begin to hear of Robert, long before he became a bishop.

One day Lambo came home with a bundle. "Ah," said Mrs Lambo. "Tea."

"No," said Lambo. "It's a young one of them, and it threw a stone at me. I thought that if we kept him a few days, like seventy of their years, we might teach him to be polite." He held out the conker for Mrs Lambo to see.

"I cannot stay seventy years," said Robert. "I am going to

be an engine-driver." That is what all bishops think when they are young. "Besides, I didn't do it. It was another boy. I am a conservation freak."

"I'm sure it's so," said Mrs Lambo. "He looks too good for tricks like that."

"I'm sorry, boy," said Lambo. "I must have made an error. But stay the night, and I'll take you home tomorrow."

And he threw the conker away. It landed just outside the palace where the bishops live, and grew there beside the sploshy mud of the marsh.

"Look, Mummy," said the little Lambo kids, "he hasn't any fur. He must get dreadful dry."

"Hush," said their mother. "He can't help being different." But all the same she smiled pityingly at Robert, not blaming him too much.

Robert played LeapLambo with the children, and games called Splash and Puddle. He was glad that for once the Mummy thought it was a good thing. Then he leaned on Mrs Lambo while she told a story. He could not understand every word, but it made the babies laugh.

He went to sleep in comfortable mud, with a Lambokid either side. Mrs Lambo sang them all to sleep with a gurgling marshy song.

In the morning Lambo took Robert home. Robert knew his address, where the house was, the number of his telephone, his postcode, but had no idea which drain to catch to get there.

It took them all morning. On the surface a whole city was searching for Robert. Under the surface Robert was coming home. Lambo loved to show the scenery, and they went the pretty way, by the Thames Undersump, the South Circular Sewer, and the Trafalgar Sinking Column (just under Nelson), the Whitehall Overpass (very far below the street), past Leicester Square again in the Double Plummet, which loops the loop, and way, way, under the greensand to the Camden Siphon, full of old stories, and into undiscovered caves round Highgate.

"I know every stitch of the way," said Lambo. "It's going to be such fun at Finchley." At Finchley, of course, the canal begins, and the lock gates have to be opened and closed.

And then they were in the old mine shafts round Totteridge.

"You'll have to go up through a grating and take a look around," said Lambo. "I think we're somewhere near. I haven't been this far in the last hundred years."

"I could get out and walk," said Robert, being a helpful boy.

"I'll take you right home," said Lambo. "They'd rather know it was all a mistake."

They came out in Whetstone Stray, by Dollis Brook, went round the corner, and walked in at the door of Robert's home.

"Two monsters," said his mother. "Come for the rest of us, have you?"

"No," said Robert. "They've been very kind. It was all a mistake, you see."

"I'm sure I'm glad you're home again," said his mother, "but I'll hug you when you've washed. There's something about you called mud."

"I'll be off," said Lambo. "Now I've brought him home."

"Stay and have a cup of tea," said Robert's mother. "Or would you prefer a bucketful?"

"It's kind of you, but I'd better be going," said Lambo. "I get sunstroke very easy even at night, out of the water like this. But Robert knows where we live, and ask him to call any time. And if I may I'll bring my youngsters round some day to play with yours. They don't get out very much, because marshes aren't what they were."

"It's very kind," said Robert's mother.

They saw him to the next drain, and waved him goodbye. Then Robert rang up the police. "They'll be worried," he told his mother. He told the police he was home.

He went to school that afternoon, but Lambo kids never go.

Blackfriar, Whitefriar

"Where have I got to now?" says wandering Jolly Jack, at Ludgate, looking up the hill at London city. "What a monkish town."

He sees Blackfriars, Whitefriars, Greyfriars, poor friars, rich friars, preaching friars, silent friars, in their cloaks and cowls and sandals.

"I'm glad I'm not a monk," says Jack.

He hears the holy towers full of ringing bells, all the churches stiff with singing, abbey and cathedral dripping hymns.

"I would not be a monk," says Jack. "All that ting-tang and all that sing-song."

He watches all the cloisters full of thoughts, and work, and prayer.

"That's not the life for Jolly Jack," says he.

He smells the kitchens full of things to eat, the cellars cool with wine.

"I hunger and I thirst most particular," says he. "And every day. Perhaps with winter coming on I'll be a monk a while until I'm full again and strong."

He goes past the Whitefriars' door that is most unwelcome shut. He comes to the Blackfriars' gate that is inviting open.

In he goes, Jolly Jack, to be a monk. They laugh in Heaven above; they think it is a joke.

"Yes," says the Prior of the Blackfriars, "please stay and be our Brother John."

There with the friars he stays, at work and prayer and singing in the choir. He has a cloak and cowl of black, and sandals for his feet, and every day he has his drink to drink and pleasant food to eat.

But often he would peer beyond the cloister garth, and wish himself still homeless Jolly Jack, beyond the wall and free but cold.

"It's winter now," he says. "I'll say my prayers a little longer where it's warm and dry."

Springtime comes, and Ascension holiday. Out go the monks to visit round the town, to gossip with their neighbours and saunter up and down the Strand or view Saint Paul's.

What with this, and what with that, friends from far away, a fairground by the River Thames, freedom and coins to spend, there is a sorry change.

Brother John leaves the cloister.

But Jolly Jack returns.

"I hunger and I thirst most particular," says he. He goes into the kitchen to prepare himself a meal.

The Prior's whitest bread, the Almoner's cheese, the Hospitaller's butter, and at last the Cellarer's keys.

"I'll open up the vault with these," says Jolly Jack. "What harm can be in going that way to bed?"

Down he steps among the butts and bottles, and looks at the display.

"It can't be wrong," says he, "to try the ale. I'll turn the tap and taste a little here."

He likes it very well.

"It would be sin to leave the wine," says he. "I'll draw a cork and taste a little there."

He likes that better still. A little more, he thinks, to make certain of the matter. And a little more he drinks, and yet a little more.

In a corner he sits down, with jug and mug, to sing a hymn or two, and then some noisy wanderers' songs, not heard by friars before.

When the Prior comes back, the Almoner returns, the sick call for butter, and the Cellarer for his keys, they hear down below the most unmonkish songs. They think the naughty devil has got in.

They find Brother John singing in his sleep.

"Disgrace," cries the Hospitaller.

"Gluttony," wails the Almoner.

"Thievery," shrieks the Cellarer. "Our sweet wine."

"The punishment is written in the Rules," the Prior says. He sends for what they have to use.

They deal with Brother John in the severest monkish way. Bricks they bring, and mortar, a loaf of bread, a jug of water.

They haul him out, take away his cloak and cowl and sandals, brick him up within the cellar wall, shut the door and leave him to his fate, a serious warning to all.

Says the Prior, "We should not have let him in."

They forget that close next door the Whitefriars live.

When Brother John awakes inside his cell with shocking painful head, he begins to kick and cry and shove. When he pushes a stone it falls, and when he tugs a beam it breaks. Into the next door vault of the Whitefriars tumbles Brother John, and wonders why he is not dead, a sorry monk he is.

They take him in, those kindly monks, and will not let him go. "Stay here with us and be devout, in cloak and cowl of white."

He stays, the summer and the winter long. He learns his prayer, he reads his book; he thinks he quite forgets his wanderers' songs, but knows his psalter through.

All is well until Ascensiontide comes round, when all the monks go out on holiday.

Brother John goes out again. And by the river something plays ducks and drakes with his devotions.

Back home comes Jolly Jack, his clean white gown all daubed with mud, his hood awry and torn.

He has forgotten every rule. He creeps into the cellar cool with all his holiday thirst. He opens up the corks down there.

"I'm dry," he says, "and first things first." He fills his jug, and tips it into his throat.

He sings 'Alleluia', and 'Hic, hic, hooray'.

The Whitefriars' Almoner hears from his study, and sends down to know; their Hospitaller sends down for quiet; their Cellarer goes to look; and the Whitefriars' Prior sends out for bricks and mortar, a loaf of bread and a jug of water.

Jolly Jack, or Brother John, asleep and singing a naughty song, is walled up in his underclothes to die at leisure, a warning against immoderate pleasure.

"Hey ho," sings Jolly Jack. "Hey ho for the poacher's life, and kissing all the girls."

His head grows clear, and he wakes. He opens his eyes and finds it dark, and hard stone in this party wall. So he sings 'Now I Lay Me Down to Rest', though there is no room to lie down. And his head aches.

In the Blackfriars' cellar the Cellarer hears him, and tells the Almoner, who sends word to the Prior.

The Prior sends for chisels and crowbars. They burst down the wall put up last Ascensiontide.

There is Brother John, blinking, but fat and well.

Beside him a loaf still fresh that should have been a year stale, a jug of water that has not dried up.

And most of all their own Brother John, walled up for a year but still alive.

"It is a miracle," says the Prior. "Brother John must be a Saint."

"It is a miracle," says Brother John to Jolly Jack. "We feel a little faint."

The Blackfriars take him back. The tale, that he survived a year walled up with nothing swallowed, goes out from London and through all the land. So by next Ascension holiday our Brother John is Prior.

"A monk I'm bound to be," he says, "in all this ting-tang and sing-song. If I hunger and thirst quite moderate it's no bad life for me. As for Jolly Jack, he shall have his joy in Heaven. I hope it is a joke he can appreciate."

"Amen," says Jolly Jack. "I see I'll have to wait."

The Ship of Angels

The first signs were found by Moorman, the verger at Westminster, who began to come across dust in every corner of the Abbey, more and more dry dust. He found it not enough to flick the particles from the priors lying hard on their stone beds, the great and awful kings with their awful lions head and foot, the slightly wicked king beside his petite queen, the warrior prince under his canopy, asleep on his last campaign, his achievements and a change of clothing high above him.

They were making the dust, he thought, as if they had stirred, shaken their heads, and were waking.

He tipped the dust out of doors in the Dean and Chapter workshop, where the lads teased him about dandruff.

"You remember what happened to the children who mocked Elisha," said Moorman. "The bears got them."

But the lads only laughed, they say.

Mr Trotter, who looked after the stonework and the drains, had no reason to give Moorman.

"It's like it was falling down," said Moorman. "Or He, you know, was blowing with His wind."

"There's nothing out of place anywhere," said Mr Trotter. "The triforiums are squeaky clean, you could wrap your sandwiches in the aisles, the clerestory you could eat out of."

"I believe it's falling apart," said Moorman. "It's the traffic."

It has always been the traffic, nowadays with buses and taxis, or five hundred years ago with drays and donkeys.

"None of the vaults is cracked, and there's no plaster come off," said Mr Trotter. "It's nothing in my line. Maybe you are doing your work right at last."

Later that evening the Precentor was walking along the south side of the cathedral, where the public don't get to, the sun on his back, wishing for a little breeze to cool him.

All at once he put both hands to his stomach, and bounded over the lamppost that is outside the south transept. He landed on the grass, on both feet, still clutching his stomach, and made two more bounding leaps, fully twenty feet into the air, forty feet along the sward; and after another ended in an ilex tree, and stayed there, thinking he must look like Zachaeus waiting for another donkey.

In due course he climbed down and went home, remembering that something had become caught in the belt of his cassock, and then jigged him up and down like a conker on a string. Mrs Precentor took an acorn from his hat and led him to his supper. But by then he felt orbitally sick and went to bed.

Moorman heard about it the next day. He had already called Mr Trotter so early and so urgently that Mr Trotter rode into the nave with his hat on, no cycleclips, and eating a piece of toast. But some say he rode his donkey in and chewed a beetroot, and others an ox, and drinking mead.

"Now, lad, what is it?" he asked

"The foundations have been cast down," said Moorman.

"The floors. Look at 'em."

Mr Trotter leaned the bicycle, or the ox, against the Dean's chair and looked about.

The diamond-shaped flags that made the great floor of the nave, instead of lying flat like an ironed golden counterpane, were all tilted and showing their edges, like the scales of a fish.

"And that's just here," said Moorman. "Come up the east end."

Mr Trotter followed Moorman to the tomb of the warrior prince.

The tomb was built like a stone table. Now it had tipped itself up, lifting one end from the floor. The top was empty, the armoured figure gone, as if it had walked stiffly through the night, clutching a long and sharp sword. In the space below was a darkness that looked as if it might ooze out.

"He's sleepwalking," said Mr Trotter. "If you see him don't waken him or he might die of shock."

"The Kings are up and about too," said Moorman. "Look."

The double bed had heeled over to one side. Below it was the dust of time, and something that looked like a royal chamber pot under the stone valance.

"They're all getting breakfast in town, no doubt," said Mr Trotter. "We'll have to tell the Precentor, and the Precentor can tell the Dean and the Dean can tell the Chapter."

They met the Precentor on the grass. "Take care," said the Precentor. "Something here pitched me head over heels yesterday and threw me into that holm-oak tree."

"Something in the Abbey has lifted flags in the nave," said Moorman. "If I can't sweep them it's not my fault."

"But everything looks right from here," said the Precentor. "Nothing falling from the fabric, I hope," he added.

"I'd never allow that," said Mr Trotter. "It's all happening on the ground, or under it."

"We'll look outside first," said the Precentor, nervous about going in and seeing strange things.

Several things had happened outdoors. Moorman had not seen when he first came to the building that morning that the lawns were cratered and mounded, and forgotten vaults were showing after centuries of burial.

"Someone is messing about," said Mr Trotter. And something invisible knocked his hat from his head, then tripped him up when he bent to retrieve it.

The something pushed at Moorman, and he laid hold of it, unseen as it was.

With gaping mouth he turned to the others. "It's a rope," he said, grasping the invisible thing. "Like the bell rope of a ten-ton bell. I can feel the strands. I can feel the fibres. It's wet." He sniffed his hand. "Seawater," he said, tasting a finger with his tongue.

"I shall report it to the Dean," said the Precentor, deciding not to join in this joke.

"It's right enough," said Mr Trotter, putting out his hand too, holding something so large that one hand would not go round it. He put two on it. Then he lifted himself up from the ground, supported on this nothing.

It swayed under his grasp. Then it lifted him higher, and he let go. As he touched the ground his hat was knocked off again and the ilex tree shook and rustled, some way ahead of them.

"Something alive in that holly bush,"
said Mr Trotter.

"Floating," said Moorman. "A thing
like that can't float."

An angel, thought the Precentor.
To think that should come in my
time! What will my poor wife say?

The thing in the tree was bigger
than it. It was more nearly the tree
being in the thing whose metallic
sides and curves were cased in
sea rusts.

"An anchor," said Mr Trotter. "You
don't get a lot of those in cathedral work,
but there's one at, where is it? Pevensey."

"It must have fallen out of a . . ." said the Precentor. But
he could not say what he meant. This very thing had
plucked him from the green and dashed him into the ilex
tree.

"Out of a ship," said Mr Trotter. "That's where they have
them."

"But here isn't where they have ships," said Moorman.

"It looks very like an anchor," said the Precentor.

"So do anchors," said Mr Trotter.

Moorman still looked upwards. But he dropped his eyes
again, seeing more that he could not believe. "Not here," he
said.

Mr Trotter looked up so hard his hat dropped from the
back of his head.

They all had to believe.

The ship lay alongside a window high in the south

transept, its deck level with one of the walkways, and the cable of the anchor hanging from its bow.

It was joined to the building by a gangway, and the gangway was letting passengers on. The first of them were in cloaks with hoods.

"Monks. They were a rum lot," said Moorman.

"Coming out of the choir roof," said Mr Trotter. "Forever of them. Why? Who are they?"

"Why aren't we drowning?" said the Precentor. "We must be under water."

"There'll be problems with the fabric if water gets in," said Mr Trotter, jangling out his cathedral keys. "I'd better have a word. No time for Dean, or Chapter, or anything else."

They hurried in through the nearest door, up an ancient stairway, into air thick with centuries of stagnation.

In the great cave of the choir roof the air was suddenly full of salt and spray, and it seemed that water washed the leads outside.

The Precentor thought he saw a familiar figure leaving through the low door to the roof outside.

"The prince," he said. "In armour. But how?"

"They've been waking these last two weeks," said Moorman.

"He's got out," said Mr Trotter. "Tired of being in one spot, an active lad like that."

"Shall we see the ship sail?" asked the Precentor. "I believe it exists. We must hurry outside again."

Outside, the ship's sails were hoisting like silken copes, under flags curved and heraldic, and a figurehead of the lion of Judah, its trumpeters four archangels.

Under the trumpets were the plain square notes of the monks; the sailor sang a rough shanty of God's weather; the saints aboard carolled a high descant, and above them the royal tones of a king lifted a melody, and the evangelic trumpets blew a blending line.

"That song, that music; how can I remember it?" said the Precentor. Precentors oversee the music of abbeys. "Who on earth could sing it?"

"There's only one ship," said Moorman. "There will only ever be one ship."

"We'll never see it again," said the Precentor.

The ship rose and fell on invisible waves. A wind from the south-west pulled the vessel on its way.

"Ahoy," sang out Moorman. "I've done with sweeping the tombs of saints. I'm going with them Ship ahoy, wait for me."

Then he was swimming through mid air, with the sweep of the waves making his cassock billow out, through trough and crest. The men, or the souls, and the angels at the ship's side let down their ropes for him, and he climbed the black and white side, and the ship turned then for her final port.

"Amen," said the Precentor.

∽ *Forbidden Music* ∽

Once there were sad times in London, and in the whole land. There was no king, and there was no queen, but soldiers in charge, who didn't know what folk wanted. You did what they told you, and thought the right thoughts even in your dreams. You daren't say how miserable you felt.

The soldiers put their horses inside St Paul's, so they couldn't believe in Heaven. They thought of pulling down the church. The spire had fallen long since, but there used to be music in it. Now men came to buy the lead roof. Lead was useful, they said, and music wasn't.

The soldiers cancelled Christmas; it was just another day with no name of its own. You got fined for calling 'Happy Christmas' to a neighbour.

But the City Waits began to remember going round to all the houses and singing, playing tunes on their band instruments. My Uncle Robert was one of them, and my father used to be, but dropped out before they cut off the King's head. I keep remembering bad bits; but those were terrible times.

Uncle Robert came round to say the Waits were all going out, never mind the guards. "God made us for singing, brother John," he said. "We must not forswear Christmas for a set of dowdy soldiers."

"You'll be singing in the jail," said my father.

"Never," said Uncle Robert. "All our family is going out with them, and we're going to warm up Christmas Eve in the streets round about."

My father said he was going to stay home and wait for better times.

"You have to bring better times along," said Uncle Robert. "There'll be no fuss, John."

"Tell me that when it's over, Robert," said my father, not knowing what would happen. No one did.

I was soon again at Uncle Robert's house in Pudding Lane, to see my dear cousin Emma, so pretty and sweet, and I did love her. So what happened broke my heart nearly, in spite of its beauty.

Uncle Robert had been up in his loft for the instruments of the band. He had hidden them when the soldiers began to take the rule over the country. Now he was sure he would come to no harm, and he had the sackbut out, the crumhorn, two violins, a hurdy-gurdy, side-drums, long-flutes and side-flutes and a fife, two horns, an English guitar, and a hautboy, sometimes called a wait.

They were on the table, being dusted and brightened, and the violins getting strings on, and Emma cradling the guitar, which she played best, picking out notes with her thumb. The little ones were puffing dust out of the flutes, and the baby setting to with the drum.

I wasn't going to get a word from Emma, so I came away. "Next night but two," said Uncle Robert. "We'll be on the streets from dark until the watchman calls ten." His two twin boys blew the horns at me like cows until he sent them in.

My father said, "You're not to go. There'll be trouble out of this. I don't want to be the wrong side of the Puritans, or I'll get no work."

But I felt it was right to go where I could see my cousin Emma, and I couldn't help it that the music was there as well to brighten the streets. Ever since, though we can have music now, I never hear it without my heart turning over, part sad, but a little touch of joy.

Uncle Robert set his band to go from house to house and cheer the folk up. They were glad to see Waits, and brought out good things for players and the children. I watched from the street end and saw them bite into warm pies and take sweet drink.

All at once there were horses hurrying, men shouting, and a clatter of pikes and swords. The music stopped with a squeal, and shouting began.

The city watch had come, and a troop of soldiers, and there was trouble. My uncle was in the middle of it, and not taking it easily. There were blows struck, and fighting on its way. But one man, a few neighbours, and a flock of children, were no match for soldiers and the watch.

In a few moments all the musical instruments had been taken away, and my cousin Emma was in tears. "Don't break it," she cried out, handing over the English guitar. I wanted to help, but I could not get past the men.

"We shan't break it," said the captain of the watch. "We have a better thing in mind."

It was a worse thing he had in mind, but his opinion was the strongest. In the street, straight on the cobbles, the men got a fire going, higher and higher, roaring into the dark sky and sparks going up the wind. You could see to the stars.

Uncle Robert and the other Waits were surrounded, and the soldiers and the watch talking to them severely. Uncle Robert turned away and coaxed his musicians into singing a Christmas song. I heard it coming and going in the breeze.

The fire glowed brighter all at once, and the singing stopped. Now the watch had a big enough blaze they were throwing instruments on one by one, so that they curled and blackened.

A shawm was first, and then Uncle Robert's sackbut. They burnt in the embers with bright flames, and I thought I heard them sound a note as they went. I told myself it was fancy, but it was more than that, because out of the fallen remains of the shawm and the sackbut, out of the flame and the ash, there rose two birds, crying out birdsong, rising and flying up in the smoke, circling and calling overhead.

Two side-drums were buckling with heat; from them birds burst like game birds on a moor, whirring and clattering, shouting up into the sky; two violins were like larks calling in the night; the crumhorn was harsh as a

swan; the hautboy a creature calling in a marsh; and the mandolin plucked and chuckled as it grew wings and went aloft.

"But this is sorcery," the captain of the watch began to shout.

"It is miracle," said my Uncle Robert.

"Take him away," said the captain of the watch. "Take them all away and lock them up."

"I said it would be so," said my father, come to see what fire was in these narrow lanes.

He was wrong. Uncle Robert was not to be locked up. He pushed aside the men of the watch and stepped into the fire himself and stood holding out his hand for my aunt, who followed after him.

Uncle Robert went up like a goose, swimming on the flame, and my aunt beside him. Alongside them went other Waits, and the air filled with their creaking calls and the shape of their wings.

Then my cousin Emma took her brothers, the twins, and the baby, and stepped into the heat herself.

"Now then, this is too much," my father was saying. But it was too late, because rising to meet the geese and the other birds were now other winged creatures.

All at once the fire was dying on the street, and the men of the watch were going away full of shame.

From above came music they could not stop, choirs of new-made angels, playing golden instruments.

We could never eat a goose again. No one will replace my cousin Emma in my heart. That was the end of the Waits. When the King comes back we shall have bands and music on the streets again.

❦ *Charing Cross* ❦

As I was going by Charing Cross
I saw a black man upon a black horse;
They told me it was King Charles the First;
Oh dear! my heart was ready to burst.

∽ *Ace High, Ace Low* ∽

Queens, Kings, Knaves, might be wise and might be fools, there is one wiser card, or more foolish card, who beats them all. But you have to cross London to find it. And there is a second card that might beat that.

Mind you, since it all happened in a pack of cards, they say, nobody can be offended. I don't wish to be taken up and put in trouble. You can get hanged for some of this.

Now, there was a merchant of London, who started from being a boy in the street, and by this and by that he got a good store of goods and money, so much that he thought he had all the numbers of life up to ten, like a hand of cards, but he hadn't any coloured ones, no pictures, no court cards. And riches isn't enough, he must have style.

If you don't have style by nature you must marry rank. With his hand full of numbers he thought to better himself by taking a higher-born bride.

"And it's got to be a pretty card," he told his clerk. "More goods with her, and a bit grander than me starting with a market barrow."

"Like that they've mostly been played," said his clerk. "Snapped up, tricks taken, trumped, discarded."

"Shuffle, man, shuffle," said the merchant. "Deal me something."

The clerk went about his work, and then he came to the merchant. "There's a girl out Brentwood way," he said, "at Knavestock, where the father is a good county man, and has money and a title better than mister, but *she* ain't very pretty."

"If that's the best you can lay on the table," said the merchant. "Well, I'll see her."

"One step at a time," said the clerk. "You don't want one too grand."

The merchant called on the good knight of the shire at Knavestock. He found a plain, small house, and the Sir and his Lady sitting down to bread and cheese, and a girl as plain as the meal, and no servant to wait on them.

"Susan, my dear," said the old knight, "go down in the cellar and draw a jug of the best ale for our guest."

"Best?" says the girl. "Why, Father, we only got the one barrel."

"Then remember," said the father, "spile first, spigot first."

Because when you *draw* ale you first take out the spile at the top of the barrel to let the air in, and then turn the tap and when you *finish* you turn off the spigot first, and then stopper up the top of the cask.

The father said it in a shortish way, reckoning his daughter Susan had a shortish memory.

Well now, the girl was gone a long time, and in a bit they heard her wailing down below, and the lady of the house went to see what it was.

The girl was sitting on the bottom step awash with ale. She got the spile out and the spigot open, and then hit on a panic not knowing which she did first, spile or spigot, spigot or spile, and couldn't put the matter right, not knowing where to start.

Of course, if you get told, "Spile first, spigot first," you don't know the ins and outs of it. And the mother made no better fist of it, and the ale pouring out and the spile floating away.

"Do it wrong we spoil the ale," she cried, and took no notice of what was pouring on the floor all the time.

That noise came up the cellar steps, until at last the old knight got himself down there to see what's what.

He was no better at the job, between one woman telling him one thing, another the rest, till he landed on his back in the liquor, and there they all were shouting.

Our merchant, sitting up at the table, thinks all the time that something might come of the girl, not pretty, but a good carriage and fine voice even wailing.

So in the end he went down to see, and found the deck of them all ways up, and picked them up one by one and laid them straight, spigot off, spile in, but the cask empty now and none of them supped a drop.

"But," he said, "I won't take her away, for you are all three the most foolish people in the world, and I shall not come again unless I find others even more foolish."

The girl, Susan, was very sad, but the merchant had made up his mind.

So he went back to his clerk, and said, "I like the girl well enough, but they are great fools all three."

The clerk said, "We must try higher then. There is the queen's own cousin's daughter in the Queensway, and if you do not find them foolish perhaps she will do. She is richer too."

The merchant thought that the queen's cousin's daughter would have both style and manners, and greater riches were no bad thing.

He went down to the Queensway and knocked on the door. The Queen's cousin himself was beyond the door. He was a Lord, and his wife was a double Lady, and the daughter the Honourable Alice. She wasn't remarkably pretty, but Alice is a very fair name.

They were just having their cup of tea, but making faces about it because they had no milk. But they made the merchant sit down, and poured him a cup, and offered milk.

"If it is no trouble," said the merchant.

"No," said his Lordship, "the girl will go. Just a little jugful," he told her, and she curtseyed and off she went.

The girl went for a long time. The merchant's teas grew cold, and still no girl came back. Only there was a noise out beyond.

So the double Lady went to see, and the noise was greater, such a breaking of pots and the women shrieking.

"Well, I'd best go too," said the Lord at last, and off he went.

The noise went on and it got worse, for now the cow was bellowing, and the Lord shouting.

The merchant went to see. The girl was trying to get milk for his tea, but she only took out the little jug and tried to

milk into that, and the cow didn't think much
of that and trod on the jug. And when the mother
came out she had never faced a cow so close, and the
rest of the jugs were cracked and tumbled in the mud. And
when the Lord went out with a basin the cow slopped in
that, and there was no end of mess.

But all this time there was a bottle outside the back door,
delivered like it always is. It wasn't in a jug, so it didn't suit,
and the queen's cousin and his family hadn't the wit to mend
things.

The merchant went home and talked to his clerk again. "I
don't know," said the merchant. "They couldn't play the
first card, so perhaps they are more foolish than the first
house I went to. Can you do better for me?

The clerk sent him next to the King's own granddaughter.
Her Royal Highness was down by the Thames with the
royal gardeners, making a sad job of getting their dinners.

They could see birds flying in the river, and they had nets
out to catch them.

"We shall drop it over them," said the Princess. "All the birds in the sky fly too high and we can't get the net up."

So they threw the net, and they threw the net, and they got more and more hungry. They caught plenty of fine fat fish, but they threw those back.

"We came to catch birds for our dinner," said the Princess. "We shall get one soon."

The merchant tried to explain that the birds in the river were only reflections of birds in the sky, and if they couldn't catch the one they couldn't catch the other, either. Also, he asked why they did not eat the fish.

"Because they are not birds," said the Princess, and the gardeners threw him first out of the palace fields, and then into the river.

When he was dry, his clerk said to him, "That was foolishness indeed. There is not much left for you, but you may try the Ace of Spades. That will take all. They are not fools down there."

So the merchant went down to that house. He did not like the girl, dressed in black; he did not like the mother, who had silver eyes; he did not like the father, who had a long tail and a black beard.

"But I am looking for fools," said the merchant.

There was a big smell of hell and pits and fires, and the father said, "Is she not beautiful? You can have her and all the world's riches if you sign this paper. Then I will show you the fool you are seeking."

Now the merchant knew where he was and who was talking to him, and he did not want to say or sign.

"Why then," he said, "I would be the fool if I did that."

Then the father with the tail, the mother with the eyes,

and the girl dressed in black, all vanished, and the merchant was back with his clerk again.

"So what's left?" asked the clerk. "You've done this country, and the one below and beyond." Hell, he meant.

"Ace high, ace low, I know what's left," said the merchant. "There's another card I'll play."

So he played it there and then. It was the joker, which might be lucky or might not, and he listened to his heart, and went back and married the girl at Knavestock.

"There's plenty more foolish by far," he said, "and enough more wicked. But luck is as luck lies, and I can look after her, spile first, spigot first."

But at his house he draws the ale from the cask.

❧ *When I Was a Bachelor* ❧

When I was a bachelor
    I lived by myself
And all the bread and cheese I got
    I put upon the shelf.

The rats and the mice
    They made such a strife
I was forced to go to London
    To buy me a wife.

The streets were so bad
    And the lanes were so narrow,
I was forced to bring my wife home
    In a wheelbarrow.

The wheelbarrow broke,
    And my wife had a fall.
Down came wheelbarrow,
    Little wife, and all.

∽ *Thomas à Becket* ∽

Years after Thomas a Becket, Archbishop of Canterbury, was murdered in Canterbury Cathedral by some knights trying to please King Henry II, a sleeping but meddlesome priest dreamed that he saw St Thomas knock down the walls of the Tower of London with his cross.

The next year, 1240, on St George's Day, 23 April, the walls collapsed, just as the priest had dreamed.

This dream and the ruin of his castle preyed on the mind of Henry III, who was the grandson of Henry II, and really had had nothing to do with the murder.

Henry seemed to believe that the dead archbishop would come back one day and hit him with the same cross, and went about in dread of being bruised.

One of the murderers, Sir William de Tracey, was actually condemned to spin sand into ropes, down on the beach at Woolacombe in Devon, until the end of the world. The others went to Knaresborough in Yorkshire and had supper.

❧ *The Ridingbird* ❧

A t Romney Marsh they say it started in Sheppey, and
in Sheppey they say it began on Canvey, and at
Canvey they haven't heard of anywhere else, so it
hasn't happened. But they don't tell this tale anywhere else.

Tommy lived there, wherever it was. He was a cheerful
man. "I do not want much," he would say, "so it is easy to
be happy. If I have little that can be taken away, then there
is little I can lose." And he would go on his way whistling.

"Listen," people would say to each other, servants to
angry masters, mothers to weary children, "there is
Tommy, with his tune tumbling out of his lips. Listen and
be happy."

The masters would cease from anger, the children would
stop their wailing, as Tommy went by.

"He is as happy as if the ridingbird had come," they would
say. At Romney Marsh, or Sheppey, or wherever, they
expected a ridingbird to come across the sea one day and
make life rich; but what a ridingbird was they did not know,
and neither do we. Of course, at Canvey they forget this
story twice a day, but between times they expect the
ridingbird.

Tommy looked after the roads in the village, so that no
one would fall in a hole or stumble on a stone, or water

forget to run into a ditch.
He knew every corner of
the place, every door, every
gate, and each field.

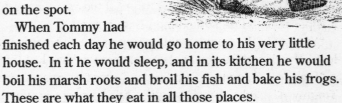

"Well," he would say, "I
should not like to lose my
work. Just if I had a little
donkey-cart to fetch up the
shingle from Dungeness."
Or perhaps he said
Wainscott Beach if this
was Sheppey; and in
Canvey they eat rubble
on the spot.

When Tommy had
finished each day he would go home to his very little
house. In it he would sleep, and in its kitchen he would
boil his marsh roots and broil his fish and bake his frogs.
These are what they eat in all those places.

"I should not like to lose my house," he said. "One day I
shall need it for ever."

Because of that, on one day a week he did not work. On
that day he walked out of the village a little way, along the
roads and paths he kept so well, to the house of a farmer.
There he would talk to Martha, the farmer's daughter.

"One day," he said, "I shall have saved enough to pay your
father the price he wants for you. Soon I shall marry you,
Martha, and take you to my house."

"It will not be long, I hope, Tommy," said Martha. "Time
is already going by."

"It will be years yet, Martha," said Tommy. "I do not

know when I shall have the rest of the bride-price for you."
He had so far gathered up one cow, one goat, and a chicken,
and that was half the bride-price, but keeping them in grain
and fodder was using up the second half of it.

"It is just as certain," said Martha, "that my father will
take a bride-price from some other person."

"That is so," said Tommy. And then he went home. That
night he did not whistle as he went. "I should not like to
lose Martha," he said. "But what can be done about it?"

The next day, and the day after that, he did not whistle.

"We have not heard him whistle," said the people of the
village. "Tommy, why are you not whistling these days? We
have nothing to keep us in peace."

"Alas," said Tommy, "neither have I. I have found out that
it is possible to lose something I have not got."

"Yes," said the people, "those things are the hardest to
lose. If a ridingbird does not come, why, we have lost that."

"I am too simple to understand what you say," said
Tommy. "I might as well whistle." But it was a sad tune he
gave.

Now there was some new gossip in the village. Up in
London, at the Tower, where the king kept his court, was
his daughter, the princess Ermenild. It was said that she
had not laughed since she was seven, when her mother died
and the king married a step-queen, nor smiled for seven
years. No prince would come with the bride-price for her,
and she was old enough to go, and what with the way she
scowled they wanted the room.

With the shortage of princes, the king now said that any
man at all that made her laugh could marry her and have
health and wealth as well. But any man that tried and failed

would be set in the fire at Smithfield.

"Any man could get out of a fire," said Tommy, who had only seen his cooking fire and not the one at Smithfield. "Not so many men become wealthy. It would be simple for me, indeed it would. I shall go, I shall whistle and, just as it is here, she is sure to smile and then of course she'll laugh."

But the simple inhabitants of the marsh were sensible enough about London, and kings, and knew what they had heard all these years. They said to Tommy, "They are not a very laughing people, and it is a bigger fire than you think. Also, if you win you will have to marry the princess and live in London, and what will Martha say to that?"

"I shall say to the king that it is simply impossible," said Tommy, "and that Martha is waiting. Is that hard to understand?"

"We understand it," said the people of Romney, or Sheppey (no one said a word on Canvey). "But kings are much cleverer."

Martha said, "I am sure it is goodbye for ever, Tommy."

"One day and another I shall come back," said Tommy. "One thing at a time is the simplest way, and I have set my mind to it."

He took the chicken from the bride-price and sold that, for a large copper coin. He took the goat from the bride-price and sold that, for a middle-size silver coin. He took the cow from the bride-price and sold that, for a small gold coin.

Then off he went with the three coins to rattle together. It was slow going for him. He was a good roadmender, and as he went he mended all the paths. It was a simple duty for him. "If it is not a good road it will not go far," he said. "And I have far to go."

On the seventh night he slept under a hedge for the seventh time. In the morning, when he woke, there was a merchant under the same hedge, setting up a market stall.

"It is to be hoped that you will buy from me," said the merchant. "I have been to the trouble of putting up my stall for you. I have only one thing to sell, and that is the egg of a ridingbird. It is very rare. In fact it is the first one I ever set eyes on."

"I had better buy it," said Tommy. "I can take it along with me. When I go back to my own village life will be rich, once it has hatched out. But perhaps I have not enough money."

"Then I shall take only a little," said the merchant. And he took the large copper coin from Tommy's hand.

"There is plenty left," said Tommy. "They will still rattle together."

He carried the egg along with him as he went to London. He had never thought that what he was told might not be true. Yet it was a sad trick the merchant had played on him, because it was not the egg of a ridingbird at all, but a great smooth stomach stone from the belly of a horse. The merchant had found it by the wayside where an old plough-horse had died. That was all the riding there was to it

In seven days more Tommy thought he heard the chick inside the egg stirring as it grew.

In seven days after that he came upon the merchant once more, with his stall by the high road.

"Is it hatched yet?" asked the merchant, when he had found that Tommy still believed the stone was an egg.

"I hear it stirring," said Tommy.

"Well," said the merchant, "you must carry it further. But now, what a happy chance that you have met me again, because I have what you will need. I have had a shipment of ridingbird saddles, quite new, and I don't know when I shall get any more."

That was not true at all, but Tommy did not know how to disbelieve. So the merchant started to sell him a thorn bush he had pulled from the wayside.

"It will soften as you ride," he said. "It is the last one of all, and luckily it will fit you perfectly."

"I had better have it," said Tommy. "But I still have not much money."

"Let me see it," said the merchant. And he took the silver coin.

"It must be a fair price and an honest man," said Tommy. "After all, he did not take the gold."

Seven days more he carried the egg and dragged the saddle, and seven days more after that he came upon the merchant again, with his stall beside the gate of London. In Romney they say one gate, in Sheppey another, and in Canvey they never left their fireside.

"Is the saddle softer yet?" asked the merchant.

"No doubt it is a little softer," said Tommy, because you have to appear wise.

"Is the egg soon to hatch?" asked the merchant.

"I believe it will soon," said Tommy, because you must be polite.

"Then I have the very thing for you, to help you along," said the merchant. He brought out a poor sickly bird, unable to fly or even walk.

"This is a ridingbird from the islands," he said. You must feed it for seven days and seven days more, and then you can ride it home. It is the only other ridingbird in the world, and when your egg hatches you will have the only two in the world, one for you and one for your bride."

"That will be Martha," said Tommy.

"Of course," said the merchant. "Such a pretty girl deserves the best."

"He knows so much," said Tommy. "I did not know he had seen Martha."

"What will you give for it?" asked the merchant.

"What I can spare," said Tommy.

The merchant took Tommy's last coin, the gold one. He said there was no choice.

"That is fair," said Tommy. "It is all I had." He did not go shopping, and did not know about change being given.

He took the drooping bird, the bezoar stone (that is its name), and the thorn bush, and went on into London Town. He was carrying a ridingbird, an egg of the ridingbird, and its saddle.

"Direct me to the Tower," he said. "There are more roads here than I have ever seen."

And he never saw so much rubbish and disorder. But, he thought, this is how the rich folk live, bless them. There is a price to be paid for everything.

He came to the Tower. "I have a good hope," he said, but the walls were high and black and the windows small, and his hope was smaller still.

At the Tower gate the egg twitched in his arms, the saddle switched from his back, and the ridingbird pitched into the dust.

"Come now, bird," said Tommy. "I should be riding you."

Tommy had to wait his turn to try to make princess Ermenild laugh. In front of him there was a juggler, who went in surrounded by bouncing balls. He came out surrounded by guards, and was taken to the fire at Smithfield.

Tommy tried to whistle a little tune to cheer himself. But his throat and his lips were dry, and no sound would come.

"Next," shouted the porter.

"Let another go first," said Tommy. But there was no one else there.

"Next," shouted the sentry.

"I'll come back tomorrow," said Tommy, not wanting to be first behind those dark walls and little windows, and last to Smithfield.

"Next," shouted the chief guard. "If he won't come, chop off his head."

"I'd better go in," said Tommy. "I'll try, that's all."

The egg rattled, the thorn-bush saddle rustled, and the ridingbird opened an eye to drop a tear.

"I shall do my best," said Tommy. "And if they send me to the fire I need not work again."

He went in. The king sat on a throne. The step-queen lay on a couch. The princess Ermenild kneeled on a cushion.

"How sad," said Tommy, "how sad she looks. No tune would make her smile, no notes would make her laugh. What can I do?"

He went to her and knelt down, but on the hard floor. "I came to whistle," he said. "But I see it won't do."

"We've had all that sort of thing," said the princess. "It won't do at all."

"I understand," said Tommy. "I shall give you my presents instead, because I am going to the fire and they are too good to go with me. First there is the egg of a ridingbird," and he put the great smooth egg at her feet.

The egg twitched and turned and moved and cracked, and split in two. It was empty inside. There was no ridingbird chick.

"What a stupid joke," said the princess. "There are no ridingbirds at all. I do not know what that is, but I see them every day."

And she did not look sad any more, but only sour.

Tommy pulled the thorn bush from his back. "This," he said, "is a saddle for the ridingbird."

"You are a simpleton," said the princess. "That is a thorn bush. It will burn very well with you in the fire. You should not have come."

And she was not sour but proud.

"There is just this left," said Tommy. "It is indeed a ridingbird." He knew it must be so, because the merchant told him. He lifted it up. He stretched out its neck, he put its feet upon the ground, he spread out its wings.

"A horrid thing," the princess said. "A vulture, or some such fowl, and dying too, I think."

And she was not only proud but angry. "Take them all away," she said. "It is no good."

But the ridingbird grew stronger. His claws scratched on the floor, his wings began to move, his crest to spread, his eyes to open and to look. He raised himself high, and was prouder, angrier, than the princess, and he called the call of the ridingbird.

"Do not do that," said Ermenild.

Then that was all over. The ridingbird began to die again. His head began to droop, his feathers to fall out; he seemed to speak, but not a word would come.

"There is no such thing as a ridingbird," the princess said. And then she said, "Oh!" and opened her eyes wide. There was a sudden sound never heard before. "What was that?" she asked. "I do believe I laughed."

She had laughed, with surprise, because as the feathers fell from the ridingbird he changed before their eyes. It was not a sickly bird that stood there now, but a strong, upstanding man.

"I have been enchanted," he said. "I was a cruel prince and lost the trust of all my people, and was changed into a bird that does not exist. I could not return until someone came to believe in me. Tommy has believed in me."

"If you tell me it I will believe it," said Tommy. "But I see you were not an egg, and you had no saddle. All the same, you are before me now."

"Prince," said Ermenild, "you have made me laugh. So you may have me as your wife."

"Ah well, it is a happy ending, I suppose," said Tommy. "But I did not make her laugh, so I must be burned. Let me whistle first and I will go quietly to Smithfield."

When he whistled the first tune, the egg of the ridingbird, or the bezoar stone, turned about and about where it lay on the cold floor, and grew, and crumbled, and hatched, and before the tune had finished a donkey stood there.

When Tommy whistled the second tune the thorn bush turned into a donkey-cart.

"Well, he shall not go to the fire," said Ermenild. "He brought the thing that made me laugh."

So Tommy went home to his own village, whistling his third tune. The prince and the princess, and the king and the step-queen, filled his cart with rich things with their own hands.

When he got home it was hard for a simple man to know how to give only two cows, only two goats, and only two chickens as the bride-price for Martha, because he had so much wealth. But it was so.

And Martha said, "Now you will stop home and have a wife."

"Indeed," said the people of the village, "you would think the ridingbird had come." And Tommy whistled and kept them at peace with one another.

You will know his village, for the roads are best there. But do not say much, because they all think it started somewhere else, or not at all.

What happened to the merchant no one has heard. He is richer, or poorer, but no better and not much worse. So it must have been Canvey Island after all.

∽ *Whoever It Is, Whatever They Are* ∽

There were men from Ireland long ago came into London and fancied they would live down by the river, sure, on a little island called Frog Island, just left lying in the edge of the River Thames for them.

There might have been folk living there already, and didn't get asked about it.

So in a while there was a man on Frog Island with the big problem, that you've never heard like it. Fergus was the name he had, but he never knew the name of the problem. He had a dog called Kerrin, and the dog didn't know at all either.

On Frog Island Fergus had a farm. It was no big place, just a building or two, and one of them was the house, and a field or two, and one of them was the garden, and a beast or two and one of them was the dog, and there was just one of Fergus and neither of them was his wife, for he hadn't one.

"There's nowhere to put it," says he, when they asked him. And maybe the fact was that no London girl was out of her mind enough to come to Frog Island, for there wasn't much about the place, and that's a fact. There was even less when the cow went dry.

"Well," says Fergus, "I don't mind about the milk, but

there's no butter and no cream and no cheese and no whey for the dog."

So they went hungry a day, and then Fergus calls in his neighbour Sean.

"Now, Jawn," says Fergus, "what ails my cow?" And they look at her, and see she's healthy enough.

"She's a fine red cow," says Sean, "and if she was a black cow she'd be a fine black cow. But would she give milk?"

They argued about that, but it got them nowhere, and it's just as well they didn't wonder whether she would be a better cow if she was green, for no one could settle that.

Sean thinks the cow is getting milked before Fergus wakes, night and morning.

"And by what, Jawn?" says Fergus.

"It could be one thing or another," says Sean. "But neither of them has a name."

"It's that, is it?" says Fergus.

"That, or the other," says Sean.

"And I've heard, Jawn," said Fergus, "that there's only one thing worse than either, and that is the other."

But they didn't know what they were talking of. Frog Island is a bit out of the way of things. Except of course for things that milk the cow.

And how would two innocent but friendly fellows from Ireland know who else had come to London?

They settled it that Fergus should stay awake the night through and watch who might be milking the cow, and find out all the matter, and maybe deal with it.

So they watched, him and the dog Kerrin, sitting on the dry bracken in the next stall to where the cow was, and her wondering what it was all about and eating her hay. Fergus smoked at his pipe and the dog was sitting on all four legs waiting for a big event.

Now the cow slept well, but not the rest of them. Yet it was a quiet time, for all that, until early morning when something comes up out of the floor, hump, push, pull and stand, rub hands and smack lips, and begins to talk to the cow.

So at that moment Fergus got himself up and banged on the stall with his stick, and the dog Kerrin goes over the partition and chases something out. They don't see it, but they think it was black. And the cow kicks them both.

When Fergus came to milk her she was full again, not a bit dry, so there was milk for drinking, for butter, cheese and cream, and whey for the dog.

"I have had a visitor, Jawn," says Fergus to Sean.

"And is the matter settled, Fergus?" says Sean.

"Well, no," says Fergus. "Not just at present."

"Ah," says Sean. But they mention no names, and shake their heads with the worry of it.

The next night Fergus sits up again. But this night there is no visitor into the cow's stall.

"Then that's that," says Fergus, when he had milked plenty of milk. "We'll have a dish of taties with our milk."

When he goes to dig the rows, what does he find but the potatoes gone, and while he watched he saw the plants being pulled down into the ground, all the whole tops of them.

The dog ran on and drove it away what's doing it, under the ground, whatever it was. But all the tops had the potatoes taken from their roots, and nothing in the black soil at all.

Fergus called to his other neighbour Seamus to see what had happened.

"What is it, then, Jawms, do you think?" says Fergus.

"I never heard of this before," says Seamus. "I wouldn't believe it at all even if it was happening, would I? But something is doing it. Or something else."

"Indeed, Jawms," says Fergus, "I'll not choose either."

"But what I think," says Seamus, "if it's any comfort, is this. It would have been the same if these potatoes had been leeks or cabbages."

"Then it's a good thing I planted potatoes after all, Jawms," says Fergus, "or I'd have lost the leeks or cabbages too. But I suppose the truth is I've company out in the field."

"That's it," says Seamus. "And they're boiling their own spuds."

That night they watched the potatoes, with the dog to run along the ridge and bark.

In the morning there were the potatoes, but the red cow was milked as dry as a rock, not a drop in her.

"At least we have a tatie," says Fergus. "We'll wash it down with the water it boils itself in."

It went like that, night about, one for the potatoes, one for the cow, and it was no time for eating or sleep.

The times they watched with one in the field, one with the cow, well, all four eyes of them closed and they got nothing.

"Whoever it is," says Fergus to Kerrin, one hungering day.

"Whatever they are," said Kerrin to Fergus, which he does by wagging his fine bushy tail.

"That too," says Fergus. "We'll catch it and we'll take it

and put it somewhere far from Frog Island, and it can go
bother the British Government, not you and me."

That day he spends his time on two things. One is getting
out his boat ready to row off to Westminster; and the other
is putting together wood, nails, wire, a cartwheel, and a bar
or two of iron and a bag of stones, a spare gate and a
grindstone, a hen-coop and a scythe, and a great old hay
rake; and there he's made a trap to catch the thing with.

"There could be two of them," says Sean.

"I'll set it twice, Jawn," says Fergus.

"There could be a pair," says Seamus.

"There's today and tomorrow, Jawms," says Fergus.

"They could be man and wife," says Sean.

They are great comforts, these neighbours. No wonder
they had to be leaving Ireland.

"I've put in a pair of doors," says Fergus. "They can come
in together. So now I'll set the trap and go in to bed."

Round the middle of the night there's a trampling and a
treading, a shrieking and a howl, and Fergus wished he
wasn't in bed already, for in bed was where he longed to be,
not getting out of it to look in traps.

There's a banging and a grinding, and a thumping and a
bumping.

The dog crawled in under the bed, hid under his fine tail,
and shut his eyes.

There's a clattering and a screeching, there's a yelling
and a leaping.

The dog crept out to see. Fergus crept out to hear. Sean
and Seamus come out to tell each other they don't know
what it is, and never expected to.

They all went down to the beach, where the clamour was,

where two things were getting in the boat left ready for them.

"I'm glad not to be rowing those," says Fergus. "There's visitors, and there's company, and there's friends; but never anything like that."

It was grand to have a black night, with two black things taking the boat – whichever one you started with, the other was worse.

The black things took up the oars, but the poor souls couldn't sit down to row, and had to make do standing up. Off they went, calling and yelling all manner of reasons how cruel and unkind Fergus had been to them, and why would he try such a trick, and they were off to try their luck in London and not among strangers.

That was nearly all; and off they went across the water and out of hearing.

Fergus went home and looked at his trap. He should have taken it down first, because Kerrin ran in it before him and set it off again. There was a great yelp from the dog, and out he came running.

Says the dog, "Share and share alike, whatever it is."

Fergus went in then and sees there's three tails lopped off and hanging there. One is Kerrin's, and now he has a stump only. And two of them are black tails belonging to the black creatures, and that's why they're not sitting down to row.

The tails are exhibited in Rainham Town Hall, and you can see them any day when you go by Frog Island, if you are that way.

But you are the only one that believes that the dog spoke and said, "Share and share alike, whatever it is."

"That's a fancy only," says Sean.

"I didn't hear it myself," said Seamus.

"There's strange things happened . . ." says Sean.

"But is that one of them?" says Seamus.

"I'd believe them the same," says Fergus.

Kerrin says nothing. He'd wag his tail, but it's up there in the Town Hall, and he doesn't see it twitch. You'll know him. He has no tail with him. But one of the three hung up might just move, if you look that way at it.

And any black creatures you meet with just the stumps, why, that's them, whoever they are, whatever they are.

If you see them, sit by the cow and watch her all night, and next day count your potatoes.

And Fergus, he's waiting for the potatoes to come up again, down there on Frog Island.

∞ *The Three Right Gates* ∞

Hounslow, on the High Road, there lived a young man called Peter, and once a year he would see a beautiful girl pass his door. She was so beautiful that the first time he saw he went almost out of his wits. He dropped his work.

He was a saddler, and all his small leathers and knives and needles fell to the floor. He stood up and followed the girl. When she had passed the door she went along the road and into the fields.

She went up by the round hill called the Low, and then she was there no more. He could not find her.

From that day on, for half a year, he was unfit to work or play, and could not eat or drink with pleasure, or speak with sense. His only thought was: Shall I see her this day? For if I do not, I may not live until tomorrow.

But the song says that never any yet died of such a fit, and he lived from day to day, and all the sad winter through until spring, and then she went from his mind.

By summer he had forgotten her. Then, one day he looked up, saw what he saw, threw down the bridle he was stitching, and the awl, and the waxed thread, because she was passing the door again.

He was out after her at once. She was at the head of the

street, and he was following; she was at the corner of the meadow, and he was at the gate; she was at the foot of the round hill called the Low, and he was by the brook.

Again she went from sight and was gone. Peter came running up, but she was not there, though there was nowhere to be gone to.

He spent the day in search, but he found nothing. At nightfall he went home and asked his friends whether they had seen her, and where she might have gone. When he came to his workshop an angry farmer waited for a bridle that lay half-finished on the floor.

"Who is she, and where does she go?" said Peter.

"I'm not the man for riddles," said the farmer. "Stitch and sew."

"I'd best do that," said Peter. "I'll not be full of sorrow this time; she'll come again, in a year, and then I'll speak with her."

And it was so with him. This time he was content to remain happy and do his work. Every day he thought of the beautiful girl with joy, and not with sorrow.

He waited for her, and in the summer, suddenly, she came. It seemed to him that she looked in at his door, where he was sewing a buckle on a belly-band.

He dropped all down, except his needle. I'll want that, he thought. That's my trade. For this time, he thought, he would follow for ever.

He went out of the door and followed up the street. This time he was closer, but did not seem to hurry near. When he was at the hedge she was in the headland; when he was in the hay she was in the stubble; when he was in the brook she was up the bank.

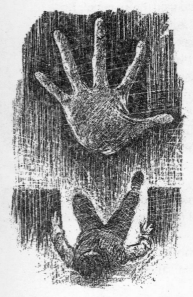

But this time he saw her at the Low. She walked about it against the sun, and before the turn was done she had gone.

"That's it then," he said, and followed her himself, against the sun. In this fashion he found himself at a gate in the grasses, a place he had not known, and a door that had never been there. He stood in the sunshine and wondered what to do.

He did not wonder long. He knew. If a door has no latch then you must knock on it. And what you next do depends on what next comes.

So he knocked. At once the door opened inwards on the darkness inside the Round Hill, and cold air ran about his feet where he stood in the summer.

BIG HAND came out and pushed him down so that he sat in the grass.

BIG VOICE said, "What is hot?"

It is a riddle, thought Peter. So the answer is not the sun, because that is too plain though perfectly right.

BIG EAR came to the door and listened.

I could make a tilt for a wagon out of that, thought Peter.

Then he thought, This is fairy business, and I'd do better to go home, for I've no defence but the needle in my lappet. But fairies keep away from iron, so I'm safe, and my business is with the beautiful girl.

But he had to guess the answer, and said, "Fire is hot, and hot is fire," because he thought that fairies hate the sun.

BIG EAR went in, BIG EYE looked at him, BIG FOOT kicked him from behind and brought him in. The door closed on him and he was in BIG DARK.

He sat in that for a time, and then there was a glimmer here and there, and he found he might be the right way up, if he tried.

He took hold of the needle for protection, and said, "Lady, where are you?"

He thought he heard her breathe and sigh. "It took you three years coming," she said. "Do you care at last?"

"I cared at first," he said. "Indeed. But you were hard to follow."

"You must come through the three gates," said the girl. "You have come through the first by answering the question."

"And where is the next?" asked Peter.

"You must answer, not ask," she said, and sighed a distant sigh, and that was all.

Then Peter could see a gate ahead of him, and a gate behind, and he had a choice of which way to go. He thought he had no difficulty, since the way to one was easy, along a clear path, and the way to the other was hard, among rocks, grass like swords, trees like spears, creatures with sharp mouths, larger creatures with claws, and greater creatures with beaks.

The choice is not hard, but the way often is.

There is nothing for it, thought Peter. I must go among the beasts and thorns. The easy path will lead nowhere.

All the same, he thought he might not live to find he was

right. No sooner had he stepped one pace towards the creatures than they began to bite.

First the smaller things he had not seen, the midges and the ants, the wasps and stabbing snakes, the poison worms, the gnawing rats. But Peter grasped his iron needle and was safe among them.

Next there came the things the size of dogs and cats, and thickets of fierce bramble, to tear his skin and blind his eyes. Then a wolf was at his throat, the ivy lashed him to a tree. He pulled away from that, and at his head the eagles flew their talons and their might. His feet tripped upon a bear, and he lost his hold upon the needle.

At once the creatures poured in on him, to crush, bite and claw. He felt his blood run down.

But the needle was safe in his lappet, and he touched it with his bleeding hand. The creatures fell away, the harsh grass he lay in turned soft and blunt, the badger licked his face, the weasel curled up like a cat. Ripe apples fell about his head; the eagles sang like nightingales.

He was in front of the gate, and light shone round it. BIG HAND opened it and sat him down. BIG VOICE said, "What is red?"

Peter looked at his hand in the light from the doorway, until BIG EAR came out again to listen and darkened all again. The blood on Peter's hand was red enough. Then he thought that fairies have another blood, it may be green. So he had a guess at the answer.

"Red is gold, and gold is red," he told BIG EAR.

BIG EYE looked at him, BIG NOSE sniffed at him, BIG FOOT kicked him through the gate. And that was that.

Now this place was too bright for him to look at, and the

high noise of it went through and through his head like an awl. But he clutched the needle in his lappet, and that was the solid quiet thing about him.

In all the noise he began to hear the voice of the beautiful girl.

"Lady, where are you?" he asked, as he had before.

"I am still waiting," she said, "the other side of the third gate. Will you come through?"

"I will come through anything," said Peter. "I will come through time, and trouble, and dreams."

"All those," said the girl.

Peter again saw two gates, darker in the bright place. The way to one was easy, down three or four wide steps.

The way to the other was a white, wide river of water, and a mountain of ice, where he could be hanged in storm and beheaded by rainbow, or be lost for ever in a wandering mist.

He took his choice and went into the raging river, where the sea-waves still ran, the wreck-waters rose and fell, and the rocks waited to grind him to salt.

He fought through the river, and climbed out among the sharp icicles of the farther bank, where the rainbows dropped their red or violet edges like razors on him, the hail sent its darts, and the snow was frozen flakes.

"Well," said Peter, "this will make my needle rusty." He found a black rock where he could polish the iron bright again, so that the snow held back, the sleet fell aside, the rainbows dropped no more, and the icicles hung steady.

There was the mist on the mountain of ice, so that he could not see. He laid the needle on his hand and walked where it pointed.

He came on to the last glacier, and to the third gate. By the time he was there, puffing and groaning in the thin air, he was able to put the needle back in his lappet.

He did not wait to catch his breath, but at once rapped on the door.

It opened, and there were green fields beyond, and perhaps he knew them. But first BIG HAND came through and knocked him down.

"I should have expected that," Peter said to himself.

BIG VOICE said, "What is love?"

Now Peter was so out of breath and weary with what he had come through that he did not remember it was the fairy people asking the question.

Straight away he said, "Love is what I feel for the beautiful girl; what else could it be?"

But as he said it he knew he was wrong.

And he was. There was BIG MOUTH and BIG LAUGH and BIG VOICE saying, "Wrong, wrong, wrong. Love is the gain of riches, the gain of gold, all works and arts. Wrong, wrong, wrong."

The door clamped shut against him and disappeared. Peter was left on top of the mountain. His good belly–band needle slipped away from his lappet, and from his hand, tumbled away down a crack in the rocks, and was lost.

"It seems to me that I shall die," he said. "It seems to me I might as well."

Then all at once the gate was there again, on the side of the mountain, and it was flinging open before he thought to knock.

Through it fell BIG HAND, and after that BIG VOICE and BIG LAUGH, and BIG EAR and BIG MOUTH, and BIG

HEAD, and last of all BIG FOOT kicked the others all helter-skelter down the mountain and followed them out of sight and hearing.

In the gateway stood the beautiful girl.

"Well," she said, "sense at last. You gave the wrong answer. But I found your needle in a crevice in the rocks, and gave the right one."

"I gave a right answer," said Peter. "Don't I feel love for you?"

"The wrong answer is the right one," said the girl. "BIG wanted a big wrong answer about love of money and of gold. I wouldn't want you if you gave that wrong answer, would I? So now let us go out of this underground world into your own."

She took him through the gate, on to the side of the Low, and the gate vanished behind them.

"All I say is, sew me down with that needle at Midsummer Eve, when the gate opens, so I do not come here and leave you, and I will be your wife and the mother of your children, and we shall be happy."

"That will be so," said Peter. And he went back to his house with her, to finish stitching the buckle on the belly-band. For the sake of it, and for a bride's present, she gave him a golden needle that sewed anything.

He's there yet, if you need a bridle or a belly-band, and she's there yet, while he can stitch at Midsummer Eve. As for being rich and having gold, well, that would be quite wrong for both of them.

∞ Silly He ∞

Up in the City, in at one of the gates, or just outside, you don't know which, there's a place you can't get to. One day Ralph was told to mind his sisters, one, two, three, and all small.

"Don't go out the gate," his mother said. Or maybe she said, "Don't go in." Wherever, Ralph did not heed, nor his sisters one, two, three.

But they could not get lost, you see, with Paul's steeple end just on yonder.

"And mind the Way-mark Man," their mother said. "Or else he takes you down the road."

There's places you don't want to be.

Then by the gate, or in or out, they played at He, and Ralph was He to start.

"It's Silly He," he said. "In strange places you must stand and stay or I'll touch and you'll be He." And so he set the rule that they were safe in certain places, silly or strange or simple.

And the Way-mark Man was not far away, ready to catch them, one, two, three, little sisters and four, Ralph, and take them down the road.

They ran about the gate and along the churchyard wall. They ran beside the Bishop's water pump and on the causey. They chased across the moat and down the alley.

And the biggest sister stood on grave of a king, and the middle on the bishop's spring, and the smallest at the very cross of the crossroads, so either they went out the gate, or either they went in.

And Ralph saw all three in line, and then he saw them go; they were not there. Where they had stood had unlocked the door into another place.

And the Way-mark Man said, "So that is how it lies. They have gone in to Paradyse."

Ralph was hunting up and down and calling, but they did not hear, until he stood himself on that same line and further off, high on Pippen Hill.

He saw the Way-mark Man come close and seek them all, and knew they were the wrong side of the City gate, for the king's grave was within the City, and Pippen Hill outside.

The Way-mark Man began to open up his bag. And Ralph supposed the sisters one, two, three, were already in, and this was for himself.

But he heard them shout with joy beneath his feet, and saw that steps led down from Pippen Hill into the ground, and light came out keener than the sun, and fragrant warmth.

He went down the steps, and there his sisters were, at play in a leafy glade, dancing with the folk, and some had hair of green and some of blue, as you well know.

On the air there was the smell of softest bread, and the breath of magic drink. The eyes of Ralph were dazzled, and his senses nearly gone.

"This is not Silly He," he said, "but Fairyland, and if they bite or gulp we here shall stay."

But the little sisters, one, two, three, saw him and began to run and still to play.

"No, come to me," Ralph told them. "It is the game no more. We are not where our mother sent us or where we belong to be."

But they ran the faster among the trees and in and out of fairy fields, and often Ralph would run and chase some creature not his sister who flung green hair in his eyes and set him off again.

"What shall my mother say?" he asked. "I did not bring them here or leave them here, but how shall they return?"

Down the steps behind him came the Way-mark Man to see the game, to wander through the fairy folk and set his way again.

And one place he marked, through which he could return.

"That is under the king's grave," said Ralph to himself. "It is a silly place."

Another mark the Way-mark Man set for the same.

"That is under the bishop's spring," said Ralph. "It is a silly place."

A third way-sign the Way-mark Man put in the grass and marked it with his heel.

"That is under the criss-cross roads," said Ralph. "It is a silly place."

"But too late now for them," said the Way-mark Man to Ralph. "They next are mine, and you alike."

And a fourth way-mark he put where Ralph had come down the steps; and that was all the ways.

Ralph was filled with dread. To escape from Fairyland was not beyond his hope. He heard it could be done. But from the Way-mark Man none ever told a story of return.

He called and called, but his sisters, one, two, three, still ran in delight of all that pretty place, and would not stay.

"Now you all are mine," the Way-mark Man told him. "On earth no more shall you be found."

Chasing three is thrice as hard as being sought. Ralph sat down on a stone to rest. He thought the game of Silly He was done, and was no more to play.

"There, we have won," said the first sister.

"He has given up," said the second.

"We shall play another game," the third one said.

"But first," the fairies said, "you'll eat and drink."

The little sisters, one, two, three, were gathered to the toadstool table where the dishes made of goblin silver stood, with on them the enchanting foods of Fairyland.

"Come taste," a fairy said to Ralph. "See, they have meat in hand."

"No, no," Ralph shouted, and leapt to his first sister and took away her cut of food. "I touch you since you do not stand in Silly He but Fairyland."

And she dropped what was in her hand, and in her turn said to her next sister, "I touch you since you do not stand in Silly He but have come to Fairyland."

And that sister dropped her bread and turned to the third, and said she, "I touch you since you do not stand in Silly He but have come to Fairyland."

And that smallest sister turned to the next beside her and laid down her crust. And next beside her stood the Way-Mark Man with open bag, ready to gather them all and take them down the road.

And she said, "I touch you since you do not stand in Silly He but have come to Fairyland."

"This is Paradyse alone," the Way-mark Man replied. "I'll taste and sup and then I'll put you in the bag and take you down the road, one, and two, and three, and Ralph, all outside the City gate." But you remember that we do not know whether it was in or out. "So now play out your last play, sisters one, and two, and three, and your brother."

The Way-mark Man then tasted fairy honey and sipped at fairy ale.

And while his tongue was glad and his throat rejoiced, Ralph took his first sister and stood her where first the Way-mark Man had marked.

"It is a silly place," he said.

"Why yes," said she, and stood there still.

The second one he stood again where the Way-mark Man had marked the next.

"It is a silly place," he said.

"It is a trick of the game," said she, yet stood there still.

The smallest one he placed where he had marked with his heel after the Way-Mark Man.

"It is a silly place," he said.

"For just a little while," said she, but stood there still.

And himself he took to the fourth way-mark. And when he stood and saw his sisters in the line, and the Way-mark Man yet at the toadstool table, in that moment the Fairyland was lost, and sisters three were safe on the king's grave, the cross-roads and the bishop's spring. And Ralph on Pippen Hill could see all three, with the gate between them and Paul's steeple straight above and high beyond.

But no more were there steps to the place you cannot reach and where he longed to go.

Then they went home and all their lives, however long or short, their hearts held the sadness of that lost land, where nevermore they went.

The Way-mark Man is still below. He touched and he took, he tasted and he swallowed. But his bag is empty now until the end of time, and there's places he don't want to be.

But stand in line with Paul's old steeple at the bishop's gate, on the king's grave, on the crossing of the roads, on the bishop's spring, and you will be there, and can follow down from Pippen Hill. But taste not, touch not, taste not, and swallow not at all.

∽ *Pippen Hill* ∽

As I was going up Pippen Hill
   Pippen Hill was dirty;
There I met a pretty miss,
   And she dropped me a curtsey.
Little miss, pretty miss,
   Blessings light upon you!
If I had half-a-crown a day
   I'd spend it all upon you.

Pippen Hill used to be outside the Bishop's Gate, leading out of the City. It was an ancient tumulus, and aligned with old Saint Paul's. When it was levelled in 1743 "certain curious implements and bones of Danish men" were found in it, but they were lost when the little museum in Houndsditch, where they were safely kept, was bombed in 1943.

∞ *Long-tail Boys* ∞

Every time Nancy come on the Long-tail Boys he get a problem. Sometimes he don't like to come out of the flat for that. Sometimes he get too lazy, because plenty of legs means plenty of body and more joints to ache, wooh!

So to save himself that much trouble he trick around all the people, and don't seem to learn any better.

The Long-tail Boys teach him a little, maybe.

He get a friend for a time, now and then, and one time he got Big Tabby. Tabby live about the place, spend a lot of time licking his feet and other places he got.

This Tabby different from the others, and he go with Nancy to the Thames and swim on those hot days and they take a picnic. Nancy like best feeling it is a holiday, and Big

Tabby never felt different from that in all his life till now.

One of these times Big Tabby take down a big jar of some good stew he got some place, with doughboys in it and real fresh meat and sausage. Nancy keep getting the smell of this jar all the way to the river, and going round and round Big Tabby on his legs to get sight of the jar.

But he saying nothing. He work round things.

Well, you going well today, Nancy, say Big Tabby at last. You making me giddy about. You going to take big swim too?

That's sure, say Nancy. I swim right up the middle of the river, and through the Tower Bridge and they lift it for me, and back again, that I shall do, man.

Big Tabby think, if he do that, my lazy friend, I do that quicker and I do it sooner and I get back first. So he say, we make it a race, and the first one back the winner.

And Nancy thinking the second one back the loser, but he say nothing about this. He say, that it, Big Tabby, we run the water race. But such good friends we are, Big Tabby, that if I don't be able to swim through the bridge with all my long legs in the narrow place, well, you won't let me drown.

I not let you drown, say Big Tabby.

And just put the jar of stew safe where Long-tail Boys and such don't get him, say Nancy.

Just in here with a stone on, so, say Big Tabby, finding a place on the wharfside.

Fine and safe, say Nancy. Now he know just where the jar of stew is, and which stone is on top.

If you just try for me, Big Tabby, Nancy say, that the arch of the bridge is plenty wide, I'll just sit here a moment and measure me, and when you come back we'll know.

We don't want you in a hard place, say Big Tabby. And he drop head first in the water and swim for the bridge, all his mind on that.

Nancy put all his mind on tipping out that jar of stew on a wood thing that floated on the bank.

Big Tabby take a look back, and see his jar all safe, and Nancy stretching out a leg another way to see how many yards across.

Big Tabby take another breath and swim on.

Nancy use four legs and put all that rich stew in his mouth, doughboy and lump of fat and slice of sausage and every little thing, and there ain't nothing left but a belch.

Then Nancy belch that belch a bit, and think, Big Tabby is on his way back, and what I done is empty out his stew.

I'll say it fell in the river, somebody done it.

But Big Tabby, he'll know that ain't true.

I tell him he never brought no stew.

But Big Tabby will remember. If I can remember then Big Tabby can remember better.

What can I do, he such a big fellow, oh man, you never ought to done that, he break every one of my bones, yes, wooh!

Big Tabby coming back now. I got that arch all paced out, he say. You come in and we'll take that race, and it's Olympics next, man.

Nancy say, maybe you don't go deep enough, all this muddy river, and the weeds, what if I get pushed down there and drowning, Big Tabby, no Olympics for me. And he think, maybe I deserve that drowning, but I had my stew.

I look again, say Big Tabby, and he draw another deep breath and swim back. He been a real friend.

But Nancy – another thing is Nancy. Nancy go off quick up to the Short-tail Boys, happy drinking beer up the street, and tell them, boys, go down along the wharf by the Tower, and dance to the song:

> I say my dinner was Tabby's stew,
>> Tabby's stew, Tabby's stew;
> I say my dinner was Tabby's stew,
>> All the fat and dumplings;
> Don't nobody tell Big Tabby;
>> Big Tabby he don't know.

Short-tail Boys they throw cans at Nancy. On your way, stumpy, they shout, and wooh! those cans bounce off Nancy's head.

So then Nancy hurry off best he can to the Long-tail Boys, all the little ones.

I tell you the new song, he say. They sing it by the river. They said you don't sing it nothing so well; it's this:

> I say my dinner was Tabby's stew,
>> Tabby's stew, Tabby's stew;
> I say my dinner was Tabby's stew,
>> All the fat and dumplings;
> Don't nobody tell Big Tabby;
>> Big Tabby he don't know.

Great tune, say the Long-tail Boys. Will there be a fight?

That just as you please, say Nancy. Could be just a fight, eh?

The Long-tail Boys they like that. When they got the tune in them head to end of tail, off they go down the river. They got a dance-hall down there and rave a bit.

I hear them, say Nancy. I hear them sing that naughty song.

He find Big Tabby real cross, real cross, down the street,

but there's nobody telling him nothing because only Nancy
know when the dinner gone, who got the stew.

He ain't saying. I just heard all them Long-tail Boys
singing about their own dinner, he tell Big Tabby. Sound
like they took all someone's, name of Tabby, they said.

Big Tabby is me, say Big Tabby. Where these Long-tail
Boys?

Sound like down by the Tower Bridge, say Nancy. You
listen good, Big Tabby.

Nancy and Big Tabby go down like friends near to the
Bridge. Then Big Tabby hear the words:

> I say my dinner was Tabby's stew,
> Tabby's stew, Tabby's stew;
> I say my dinner was Tabby's stew,
> All the fat and dumplings;
> Don't nobody tell Big Tabby;
> Big Tabby he don't know.

Big Tabby, he work his claws sharp and his tail, why it fluff
till it might blow away, and his angry throat rattle, and he
dribble with rage.

You well, then, Big Tabby? asked Nancy.

I been better, say Big Tabby. I been worse. But I never
been so tormentedly angered.

Then he knock over the ticket man and he knock over the
guarding man, and he flatten the band, wooh!

And he go for the Long-tail Boys fast as he can.

The Long-tail Boys they run up on the roof, and Big
Tabby pace about waiting for them falling off, he going to
teach them singing.

But one of the Long-tail Boys get away and tell the Short-tail Boys, and the Short-tail Boys come down the street and Big Tabby don't stand about.

Long-tail Boys and Short-tail Boys they tell Big Tabby where that song come from, but Nancy, he haven't stayed to answer questions. Nancy got sharp on his way home, up the stairs and lock up the door of the flat and wrap himself in quilt and get under pillow and stay asleep.

And he can't come out, because the Short-tail Boys they singing a new song on the landing and he don't like that new song about Nancy;

and the Short-tail Boys, they on the roof, singing an old song he don't like no better;

and Big Tabby in the street, singing what Nancy don't like to hear.

Maybe Nancy lying there yet and that stew dinner got to last him good long time.

∽ *Come Buy, Come Buy* ∽

A supermarket in the eastern part of London does not wish to be named, or even the Borough it is in mentioned. Trade has been bad enough already, quite unprofitable in fact.

"It's a good level site," said the architect.

"There's no trouble with planning and development permission," said the local authority.

"We'll bear in mind the ethnic community," said the marketing department.

"There used to be a pond with wriggling creatures in," said the environmental people. "But it seems to have disappeared over the last few years and no one can tell us anything about it."

"They should ask," said Mrs Bendixon. But she didn't live in the Borough any more, having gone even further east to a flat, and the boys were in Dagenham and the girl over the river, never saw her much.

"When I was a girl myself," said Mrs Bendixon, if you could keep her on the point. She would shake her head and look dreamy, and forget to say her thoughts out loud. Or perhaps she doesn't want to.

The building went up at the end of the new Centre.

"Used to be a little bit of woodland," said Mrs Bendixon,

the time one of the boys took her along, a day or two after it opened. They often have a few low prices just at first and think they've got you fastened in. But you can fasten anything in, if you don't look out. "Just where the toilets are," said Mrs Bendixon. "Three trees, but nothing changed otherwise, couldn't go in there – dogs and boys."

And then she went home, and didn't think about the new store.

The management and the owners didn't want her to think about it, not publicly. They wanted people to come shopping, but not to think too much, not to hear anything.

"But what did happen to . . . ?" Mrs Bendixon said to herself. "Well." Because it had been nice, though you didn't say, as well as pretty horrible. But some things might be your own fault, she decided.

At the headquarters of the supermarket chain they thought something different.

"We didn't get it wrong," they were saying, tipping ash into ash-trays, playing with edges of blotting paper.

"It is not our responsibility," they were saying at the Town Hall. "It's a private matter. Speak to the original owners."

Which didn't help, because someone had drawn a line a little thick across one place and added a bit of land in by accident.

If it's the edge of the land it doesn't matter. If it is in the middle then you have an aggrieved original owner. And an aggrieved present owner.

"It's a quarter of a hectare of prime selling space," said the Local Manager. "And somewhere in the middle, this."

But where, and what, seemed to be a problem.

"I know exactly where," Mrs Bendixon thought. "I can tell. It'll be where they put the eggs."

She had bought eggs, barn 4's, which must be healthier if they were cheap. But they had been a disappointment, which was partly why she never thought of going back to Shoppersave.

That's the name slipped out, but you probably heard of it. Mrs Bendixon may be the only person left who knows accurately about matters and why there was an expensive alteration to the store.

She never did anything about it, but the barn 4's, were strange.

You'd think they weren't the barn 4's of good English hens. Not just because they hatched, but because they didn't hatch into fluffy yellow cheeping chicks, but into another thing.

"Fancy seeing them again," said Mrs Bendixon. "It does bring it all back."

Then she blushed a bit, because Mr Bendixon never knew. He would have been cross. If she had married anyone else it might not have mattered. It might not have mattered with Mr Bendixon, but it was best not to find out, nice though he was. And too late to tell him, because he would always wonder.

But if it hadn't been for what was under the egg display perhaps it would not have been Mr Bendixon. But even if there had been sugar or yoghurt instead of eggs Mrs Bendixon would still have thought of what might have been.

At the headquarters of Shoppersave they just knew they had a problem, to do with eggs and buildings.

"Bombshell," said the District Manager.

"Eggshell," said a secretary, and nearly lost her position.

Perhaps Mrs Bendixon would have been Mrs Hampnet. It seems silly to think it, and she isn't willing to say, but she never forgot Charlie Hampnet. She didn't want to. Because he had been very handsome.

They went down to the pond when they were at the Elementary School, with a little shrimping net, and it was all about catching newts or frogs or lizards, or whatever they were.

Mr Bendixon had been at the Church Lads' meeting, and Charlie Hampnet didn't belong. Mr Bendixon wasn't to know that Mrs Bendixon (which is how he assumed she would end) was going anywhere with another boy.

Particularly Charlie Hampnet.

"I will kiss you," said Charlie Hampnet, dredging about in the little pond with the net. After all, he had been to a cinema once and seen a film, so he knew that was how men of the world behaved.

"Aow," said Mrs Bendixon, meaning, yes and no and how dare you and come on. And what do you mean exactly, because the left cheek was a girl and the right cheek was a boy, they said, and on the mouth . . . well, that wasn't allowed.

Except in the cinema, apparently. So that was satisfactory, and no harm came to her. It was nice. Mr Bendixon would have to look out for himself.

Except that the little net had caught something from the pond, and in the excitement had swung up into the air and the thing had crawled out and dropped down Mrs Bendixon's dress.

"Give up," she had said, feeling an active thing in some clammy site of passion between her shoulders.

But Charlie was down by the pond again, forgetting kisses now he had had his way.

"I lost my polywog," he shouted. "What you done with it?"

The polywog scrambled out of a woolly vest and dropped to the ground. It was very angry.

It was green. It had several pairs of legs. It had a tail like a poodle, a head that was somewhere between a crocodile and a cow, lizardy but wide, and with plenty of teeth. It had glittering claws and scales.

Mrs Bendixon was scratching her back to get the rest of them out, but that was the only one. It acted on its own. It ignored Mrs Bendixon and went for Charlie, biting him on the leg.

At the headquarters of Shoppersave, seventy years later, they were showing their wounds.

"Some of them were boiled," said a Complaints Department girl. "But they brought back some alive, and I might get hydrophobia from an unknown species."

"It's going to remain unknown," said the Department Manager (South East). "Get them all back, say it was a joke that misfired and we won't do it again, give them five pounds for each one returned and offer a thousand for the one with the lucky number on."

"But there aren't any lucky numbers on them," said someone.

"Then we save the money," someone else told him.

Mrs Bendixon never heard about the offer of five pounds. She threw away the hatching things and kept her memories. Of course Charlie stayed handsome. But he was sure that Mrs Bendixon had thrown him into the pond just for a stolen kiss. And bitten him on the ankle. With all her little teeth.

"I just stayed home and did my sewing," said Mrs Bendixon later on to Mr Bendixon. It was no good telling him she had been slightly unfaithful.

And Charlie steered clear.

And the little pondy place, hardly more than a puddle in the middle of some waste land, surrounded by the remains of prams and wooden crates, and grown over with tall red dock and thick smelly herbs, the little pond had a few tales told about it, and in the end a line was drawn through it on a plan and it was forgotten.

Until the polywog had the chance to lay some eggs.

"About forty dozen," said the National Manager. "Not to mention the cost of the rebuilding."

Because they had to take up the floor, find the damp patch, and build a sort of internal tower right to the roof, to keep the polywog in.

It got into the corned beef before they knew, and it sliced out green with teeth.

It got into the Delicatessen Dog Delight Dinners and bit the dogs. It got into the hundreds and thousands and they climbed about.

But now it is walled in and there is no more trouble.

Only Mrs Bendixon knows roughly what was there, where the place was, and at the same time almost nothing about it. And she still wonders what it would have been like with Charlie Hampnet.

✎ *Gracechurch Street* ✎

Margery Mutton-pie and Johnny Bo-peep,
   They met together in Gracechurch Street
In and out and over the way;
   "Oh," says Johnny, "it's chops today."

⚭ *The Man from Basskirk* ⚭

No one knows where Basskirk is, but a man who lived a long time there, beside the earth walls of the old fort, once was sleeping in the fields and had a dream which told him to go to London Bridge and he would be told of some great matter that would benefit him.

He put it from his mind a long time, but one day he walked to London and stood on London Bridge, with the carts and the folk going by between the houses and the river crossing under them below the stone gratings.

By the end of the day no one had told him anything but to mind to get out of the way. So he thought he would walk back to Basskirk and say nothing.

Just as he resolved that, a little old priest walking by ran against his elbow, and they got talking. The priest said he had seen the Basskirk man standing all day, and wondered why.

The man said that he had had a strange dream that told him to stand on the bridge, but he could see it was nonsense, and time to go home.

The priest said it was always so with dreams, for hadn't he dreamed himself last night that if he went to Basskirk there he would find great treasure under a black elder bush in the castle garth, and he was sure there was no place called

Basskirk, so he was not troubling himself further, and he advised the man to take no notice of dreams.

The man was struck dumb with what he heard, and knew it could not be a trick. But he managed to laugh and agree that dreams were only nonsense.

So they parted, the priest to his prayers, the man home again.

He dug under the black elder in the castle garth, the place called Borth, and no great way down he found a little pot with strange writing on the outside and gold coins in it.

So that was the meaning of the dream, and he lived in better comfort than he ever had, and opened an ale-house for company. The pot sat on the mantel for curious folk to see.

One day a traveller came in and looked at the pot and knew what the writing read in the Welsh, which was that if someone looked lower there was another pot twice as good.

The ale-house keeper once more said nothing. But that night he dug again, and far down he found another pot larger again, with more strange writing, and inside it twice as many gold coins.

So next he was the keeper of an inn and put up travellers. And one day another traveller took up the second pot and read the writing on that in the Hebrew, which said that digging deeper yet would uncover twice as much again.

The man thought there was no end to his good luck, and dug deeper again. At Basskirk they reckon he is digging yet, for he has not come up.

⚭ Shots of Simple Jack ⚭

J ack the silk weaver of Spitalfields was simple to the world, but in setting out his long warps he had more skill than he knew, and in weaving weft across and across no one had more cunning. For his yarn he chose the finest, for his dye he chose the sharpest, and back and forth the glinting shuttle shot.

The Lord Mayor and the Lords of the Land, the Judges and the Queen, all waited for his loom to bring them cloth that no one other person's soft and knowing hands could make, in colours no other eye could mingle.

But those hands, and that eye, were without any skill at money. Whether he had any, Jack did not ever know. Where he had put it he did not remember. How much there was he quite forgot. What any thing cost he could not puzzle out.

So he remained poor, because he did not take enough for his bolts of cloth, and paid too dear for the thread he bought.

"I'm paid," he would say, "when the swags of cloth fold down from the loom." And all day long he watched the patterns grow, the new stuff grow in heaps and bales.

"My only pain," he said, "is parting with it, for where it goes I never go, and whether it is happy where it goes I never know."

Because he was never in parlours and palaces or chanceries and courts. Only sometimes when the light was bad and night had come would he go to the silk-weavers' tavern and come away with all his coins spent on friends.

Or sometimes those not so friendly would sell him things of no use, and when he was home his wife would scold him.

"But Tom," he would say, "or Peter," or some other friend, "says this is what I need. So do not lose it, like the Duke of Lithuania who lost the great Holy Jewel of Vilnius crossing London Bridge the other day."

And his wife would take the thing away and say, "We need nothing to take the fishbones out of donkeys' hooves, nor do we have use for spurs, or a parrot cage. And we have nothing worth losing."

"I did not know," said poor Jack, and sadly went to work again, knowing she thought he was a fool.

"You weave," said his wife. "And I shall buy and sell, or there'd be nothing. You buy nonsense and you sell for nothing."

Jack set up a warp of tangerine, a weft of plum, and ran it through with singing birds of black and green, making a haunting cloth too beautiful to sell. He hid it well away.

"I'll sell it best myself, one day," he said. "I cannot part with it just yet."

And in a week or two he made other things. His wife loaded up a great pack on her shoulders, saying how heavy it was, and took it to market, grumbling about the weight.

When she had gone Jack found his singing birds rolled in the bottom of the cupboard, a small work but very great in beauty.

"Well," he said, "I can part with it now. I'll take it to the merchants by myself, and show her. And who knows, on the way I might find the Holy Jewel of Vilnius and get the reward and take on an apprentice and not work so hard for so little."

So he went dreaming on his way.

"You wife was here not long since," said the silk merchant in the City. "But her prices were too high today."

"That's no way to go on," said Jack. "She should sell for what she can get."

"I told her so," the merchant said. "But what have you brought me yourself?"

Jack unwrapped his parcel, and the merchant was amazed. "This beats all," he said. "I never saw such stuff." He took out his purse of money and put the gold coins in Jack's hand.

Jack was amazed. He had not seen so much money. And when the merchant had emptied his purse he closed his hand and the coins overflowed.

He picked them up, and went into the street. He could buy anything now, he understood, and he would buy the most useful thing there was.

He remembered how his wife had struggled with the weight of silk, and how she laboured to fetch and carry all the household goods and fuel. She did this because Jack must keep his hands tender for his work.

Seeing a man with a donkey, Jack said, "That donkey would be useful to me. Will you take this for it?" And he held out his money. It was more than fifty pounds.

"I'll be kind to you," said the owner of the donkey. "That will just do. Lucky I am in a good mood."

"It's all I've got," said Simple Jack, and got the donkey. "She will be pleased," he said.

"She will," said the man. "If you can get it home."

The donkey was very obstinate, and would not go the way Jack wanted. At London Wall it spread its hooves and would not go, at Bishopsgate it would not go, until Jack was tired of it.

"You should sell that," said a costermonger at his stall. "I want a little donkey." He could tell that Simple Jack simply did not know how to deal with donkeys, because the first thing you need is a stick, and the second is a bigger stick. But he did not tell Jack.

"What will you give me for this beast, then?" Jack asked.

"It would be dear at five pounds," said the costermonger. They do not trade by offering good bargains.

Simple Jack took the five pounds, and was glad to be rid of the donkey. But he still wanted to buy something to take home, the best thing he could get.

So from the very same costermonger he bought with it a sack of new potatoes, and hoisted it upon his back.

That was all very well, but he hated the coarse sacking, and by the time he got to Houndsditch the weight was too much for his back, which was more used to crouching over his work.

So he was glad to exchange the sack for a silvery mackerel from a fisherman selling his catch. It was light to carry, and the scales were shot with silver, blue, and green and like some new silk.

At home he found his wife. "I did not do a very fine trade," she said. "The prices I was offered were an insult, so I came wearily home with my load. But on the way I called at the first merchant, who told me you had been to him with a cloth of such beauty he gave fifty pounds or more. So if you hand it to me I'll go out once again and buy our supper."

"I have done that," said Jack, and showed her the mackerel. "It will do nicely for two."

"But there must be more money," said his wife. "You did not give fifty pounds for a mackerel, did you?"

"It was like this . . ." said Simple Jack; and he explained line by line what he had done. His wife was very cross to find him still such a fool.

But it was no good being cross with Simple Jack. That would not make him wise, and all he did he did for love. So she said little, but with a tear in her eye she took the fish and split it open before cooking it.

"Such a fish as this," she said, "has not only cost fifty pounds, but has ruined my best knife into the bargain." Because something in the mackerel's gut had caught the blade and damaged it.

But there, across the table, rolled a stone as big as her thumb. She picked it up and wiped it clean, and it lay shining on the table.

"A pretty thing," said Jack. "We'll have mackerel again."

"Oh, simpleton," said his wife. "That is the Holy Jewel of Vilnius, and the reward will make us rich."

"Only if you look after it," said Simple Jack. "I am too foolish."

"No indeed," said his wife. "Who else would buy such a fish? Only a wise and lucky man."

They went to the Duke of Lithuania, and he handed over a box of money.

"I shall carry it," said his wife, "and keep our luck."

"You are my luck," said Simple Jack beside her. But he was dreaming of a new fish-scale pattern and longing to be at his loom again.

∞ *Sovran Toff* ∞

Very long ago in the middle of London there was Lobrogar, him that was big and strong but slow, and "Look at him," the children cried. But he wouldn't stop.

Then there was Stobrogar in the middle of London too – and where else would they all be? – him that was shining and middle-sized and moved quicker and didn't rest.

And there was Dobrogar, little and quick and sunburnt, they say, from working so hard.

Above them all was Sovran Toff, riding in a cab, and there was never a child dared call after him, or the rest would turn and that child was no more.

Sovran Toff never went without Lobrogar, Stobrogar, and Dobrogar. It was like a club, or a gang, or a company.

Sometimes they were good, sometimes they were bad, and they were always ready for a chance, day or night. You didn't have to explain much, but they would be on to it.

"Chance is the finest thing," said Sovran Toff.

"If we do the work," said Lobrogar.

"It's understood," said Sovran Toff. "All for one, and one for all, and no change given."

Sometimes it was serious, sometimes it was a game. So one night it was time for a lark, and they had to find out what it was.

"It's swimming," said Dobrogar. "But we'd sink."

"It's boating," said Stobrogar. "Afloat, afloat."

"It's another country," said Lobrogar.

"That's it," said Sovran Toff. "The French ladies are on the river, and if we could catch their little monkey, why, that would be the lark. We'll sell it back, and that will set them cussing."

Then they had think how it was to be done. But Sovran Toff knew about that.

"The monkey hangs his tail over the side of the boat," he said. "He's fishing. Put a string on the tail and drag him to the land. The wetting will soften him. Don't be long."

Lobrogar, Stobrogar, and Dobrogar tried that, but it wasn't the best trick. Sovran Toff was along the river bank hooting at them to hurry, and the French ladies thought it was a steamer.

But the monkey wouldn't put his tail over the side. The thing is, he was a monkey without a tail.

Now Sovran Toff knew this, after the others had set off, but all he could do was stand on the bank and shout like a fog-horn through his hands.

Lobrogar, Stobrogar, and Dobrogar failed. When the French ladies came to land they went to Sovran Toff and told him, and showed him the wet string.

"I was trying to tell you," he said. "The monkey does not like fish, or else he would have a tail. So we shall have to try something else." He was a bit angry with them, and that wasn't fair.

Dobrogar was crying.

He didn't think of anything just at that time, but Lobrogar

and Stobrogar began to wonder, and they remembered what had a tail and liked fish, and all of them went to catch that, to keep Sovran Toff happy. The French ladies did not have one of those, so they had to hunt round the streets.

"Puss, puss," they were calling. But the children were roaming about too and shouting at them and setting dogs on them, and all the pussy cats went indoors, because of the dogs.

So Lobrogar, Stobrogar, and Dobrogar got off the streets, and there was a pussy in a box all ready for them.

Lobrogar could not get high enough off the ground to do anything. Stobrogar was too fat to get through the openings in the box. Dobrogar could, but he was frightened that he might go head over tail into the mud and be picked up by a stranger.

So he climbed up and picked open the lock.

And when pussy came out they hooked the wet string on his tail and tried to lead him to Sovran Toff. Sovran Toff was asleep in his cab.

You can guess they caught the King's lion at the Tower, and they were trying to lead it backwards through the streets, Lobrogar working away with his weight, Stobrogar leading the way, and Dobrogar coming up last at the bitey end of the lion.

Still, it kept the boys away, and there wasn't a dog saying a word.

But really, that didn't suit Sovran Toff, because his cab-horse pricked up his ears at the din, sniffed up the smell of lion, saw its claws and teeth, and turned left for away. Sovran Toff was tipped out and sitting in the street.

They were saved by the keepers of the lion, who came out to see it wasn't hurt and didn't eat anyone valuable, and they took it away.

"My boys are good brave boys," said Sovran Toff. "They caught up this dangering beast and held it for you, be glad."

"Being glad," said the keepers. "Come on, Leo, be good."

When they had gone, "Well," said Sovran Toff, "you are good lads, but you got it a bit wrong, that's all. So call me another cab. We haven't lost anything."

"We kept our bit of string," said Dobrogar, and there it was, wet and liony.

"Better luck next time," said Sovran Toff, getting in a new cab. "Don't bother about whether it eats fish next time, then."

So they didn't bother about that.

"We tried a small thing first," said Lobrogar. "No good."

"We tried a middle thing next," said Stobrogar.

"We'll get a good big 'un now," said Dobrogar.

There was only one thing bigger, and they got that wrong too. There it was, and it didn't like fish but turnips, and it had feet like a church and said its prayers deep in its belly.

"Up," said Lobrogar, and Stobrogar climbed on his shoulders, and "Up," said Stobrogar, and Dobrogar climbed on Stobrogar's shoulders with the string.

And he put the string on, and the thing like a mountain didn't say a word, because that wasn't the tail but the nose and it never spoke.

"Walks backwards better than that pussy," said Dobrogar.

"Got trees growing out of it," said Stobrogar, because he didn't have tusks, and didn't know about them.

"It got eyes at the wrong end," said Lobrogar. "Not a pretty sight.

They got their elephant to Sovran Toff, and his cab-horse drove off alone again. But Sovran Toff thought this elephant the best lark yet, and tried to get up on his back, and the elephant watching with eyes at one end or another.

But the elephant wasn't best pleased at any of this, and got the string off its nose. They have a handling nose.

And he stamped on Dobrogar, flat as a penny, and he stamped on Stobrogar, thin as a sixpence, and he stamped on Lobrogar, crisp as paper, and then he stamped on Sovran Toff fine as gold leaf, and went home to his turnips.

As for the others, the boys picked them up and spent them.

Pop Goes the Weasel

Up and down the City Road,
   In and out the Eagle,
That's the way the money goes,
   Pop goes the weasel!

Half a pound of tuppenny rice,
   Half a pound of treacle,
Mix it up and make it nice,
   Pop goes the weasel!

Every night when I go out
   The monkey's on the table;
Take a stick and knock it off,
   Pop goes the weasel!

∽ The Heath-mad Maid ∽

There was a farm the top side of Hampstead Heath, where it's all houses now, and the cows have gone.

There was a farmer there who had three sons, who all fell in love with the same girl. Her name was Linnet, and she was the daughter of a miller just over by Golder's Green, and the prettiest maiden in the county (but you wouldn't bother looking further), smart as a windmill and turning to all the winds.

There was a rich city merchant who was building a big house in those parts, and hadn't thought to look further for a bride, and decided he would have Linnet. So he spoke to her father, and between them they kept the local lads away.

But Monty, the farmer's eldest son, thought he might get in with Linnet before the merchant won her over, if he could just speak first.

"You'll never manage," said his father, and "Good luck," said his mother. They both thought he had only to ask, because he would get half the farm after them, and stints on the heath.

"I'll bring her back, never fear," he said.

And off he went. On his way to the mill he met the Heath-mad Maid, wild with living among the furze bushes, and probably a witch, so no one need be kind.

"Good-day, my son," said the Heath-mad Maid. "Where are you going this morning?"

Monty hurried on without replying. He thought that to speak might bring bad luck. And he was working out what to say.

But at the mill he came out with his ideas too soon, right to the question before saying "How do you do" or any politeness. He thought he didn't need that, a good lad like him with half a farm to come and pasture on the heath.

He was wrong, of course. Though Linnet liked him well enough, she only laughed at him and thought he should go, a silly with no manners. So he went home and said he'd decided against her, and his parents said, "Oh well," and wondered about Rowley, their second son.

So he tried on his own account a week or two later. They sent him off with a pat of butter to season her new bread, and a word from Monty about taking his time, which was kind of him.

Rowley also met the Heath-mad Maid.

"Whither away?" she asked. "You so hurried and carrying new butter."

Rowley went past without answering her, clutching his butter. But when he got to the mill Linnet would not take the butter from his hand.

"But I shall have half a farm and can turn sheep out on the heath," said Rowley. "I would do you well."

"There are those that have already done well," said

Linnet. But she quite liked him, did not know why she laughed, and sent him away.

"Well, close too," said Rowley, when he got home, "the miller's daughter has dust in her hair."

Then Alex, the youngest son, wondered whether he had a chance. He made a little junket in a bowl to take to Linnet.

He set out without hope. His parents told him not to trouble. His brothers told him he would be shamed worse then they were. But they wished him luck, expecting he would not find it.

"I will do my best," he said. "She is very fair to see."

"She laughs," said Monty. "And you are a fool."

"She is dusty," said Rowley. "And you have a long nose."

That was true. Alex was a strong, clever, and gentle lad, but he had a very long nose, and this, as he knew, made him look ridiculous and kept him shy. He used to wander alone across the heath rather than meet people.

So when the Heath-mad Maid met him and asked him where he was going, he knew her, and told her.

"Nowhere that will prosper me, Granny," he said. "I am about to call on Linnet and ask her to be my wife."

"And you are carrying a bowl of junket," said the Heath-mad Maid. "Will she like that as well as I should?"

"I suppose not," said Alex. "Please take it, Granny, where I know it will be liked."

"I will," said the Heath-mad Maid. "And in return look at this ring. Put it on your finger and say 'Bless it!' "

Robin did so, and his nose grew half an inch shorter, and he became very handsome and extremely cuddlesome. And this he saw in the bowl of junket.

"Now," said the Heath-mad Maid, "if Linnet refuses you

give her the ring to wear. Then every time you say 'Drat it!' her pretty nose will grow half an inch longer, and she will become ugly, and be very glad to marry you. Then you have only to say 'Bless it!' and her nose will grow shorter and she will recover her beauty."

"Will I be so cruel to do the first thing?" said Alex.

"I daresay not," said the Heath-mad Maid.

He ran to the mill, but Linnet was out. So he sat below the sail and closed his eyes. While he was asleep the rich merchant called, and saw the ring hanging round Alex's neck on a plain flax cord.

"An engagement ring!" he said. "I'll keep that out of this lad's way." He cut the cord with a silver knife, and put the ring on his own finger.

But Alex was woken by the cutting of the cord, and without opening his eyes enough to be noticed, began to whisper "Drat it! Drat it!" and as he said these words the miser's nose grew longer and longer.

"Something is stinging me!" cried the merchant, running

off to his doctor, who was down in London far. "My nose is swelling and I have allergy!"

Happily, Alex did not want his ring any more. Linnet was surprised to see how handsome he looked. Before he said a word she smiled at him, told him to come into the mill kitchen, and take a cup of tea.

"I am so pleased to see you," she said. "How ugly the merchant is when you look close."

She had always liked him for his gentleness, and she now fell quite in love with him, and agreed to marry him as soon as he got a farm. And of course Alex did not find she laughed, and if there was dust in her hair, why there was dust in his.

So he stayed all the evening, and matters were getting settled, except for the matter of the farm, because Alex would never get a half share or any gaits on the heath for cows or geese or sparrows for that matter.

All he had were the shoes he stood in.

Before he left the mill the merchant came by again, as ugly as ever. And he was more so when Alex had whispered a word or two again, which was "Drat it".

"Return my ring," Alex said, "and I'll cure you for one thousand pounds."

"Never," said the merchant. But Alex had only to whisper and his nose swelled again, until he would have given anything for a cure.

But Alex thought a thousand pounds would do, and it did. He and Linnet bought Cherry Tree Farm, where all the trees grow now. and lived happily a long time.

The Heath-mad Maid brings her junket bowl twice a year, and leaves presents for the children.

❦ *Sammy Soapsuds* ❦

When little Sammy Soapsuds
    Went out to take a ride,
In looking over London Bridge
    He fell into the tide.

His parents never having taught
    Their loving Sam to swim,
The tide soon got the mastery,
    And made an end of him.

∽ *A Packet of Silver Coins* ∽

One day, not far from the house where the old Chinaman Xeng (but he was always called John) used to live, and not far from the London docks, an officer from a ship found a little packet of silver taels, or Chinese coins, tied up with thread and mixed with pleasant-smelling ashes.

John no longer lived there, and in fact his bones had been found in his garden sitting under a tree.

So there was no one to return the coins to. So Second Mate Gordon Scrimshaw put the bundle in his pocket and went home to visit his mother and his brother, for a few days' leave. It was just good luck that they were both home together. In fact they had arranged to meet at the end of London Bridge, and cross the water together.

"I don't know what it is," Gordon told his brother Edwin, meeting him and waving his new straw hat in greeting with one hand, and showing the little packet in the other. "But I don't know either where it should go."

Now the brother, Edwin, had been a missionary in China until he got so nipped at by devils, and the Bishop of the China Seas, that he came away; and here he was. He knew what was what.

"I hope we aren't too late," he said. "But that is a very bad joss indeed, Gordon. I know something about these matters from my time in the Orient. You should never have picked it up."

"Just interest," said Gordon. "Not been stolen, or anything, has it? Shan't have a Bow Street Runner taking me before the magistrate, or anything, shall I?"

Edwin laughed at that, but not very deeply. "You did nothing illegal," he said. "In fact the coins are definitely yours now, and so is all this funny ash. The fact is that you have picked up some sort of little devil, and you have to get rid of it at once."

"I suppose it came from that old Chinaman that had the laundry all those years near Wapping Old Stairs," said Gordon. "You remember they found the bones and weren't sure about a church burial for such an old heathen."

"Very likely," said Edwin. "Look, this matter is beyond praying for. This bundle was put out for you, or someone, to pick up, and inherit some sort of imp. So how do you feel about that?"

"I feel, let's be rid of it," said Gordon.

"Well then," said Edwin, "what's that on your hat?"

There was something on there, walking about the brim, sweeping and tidying.

"They don't," said Edwin, "like," and he threw it over the bridge, "water," and it landed in the Thames and floated away.

"Well, thanks," said Gordon. "You're a man of action, even if you are a clergyman."

"Least said, soonest mended," said Edwin. "But let's not tell the bishop in case he thinks I'm superstitious."

That should be the end of the story. But the ending is sad, and will take a little longer.

Gordon had got rid of the thing he had picked up, the impish elf from the old Chinaman Xeng. The hat had floated down the river.

Then it had met the returning tide and been carried up the tideway again, under each of the bridges, possibly for many years, and at last been washed up on the shore at Hammersmith.

There it lay on the mud for a year or two, until a boy threw an apple core at it. The apple core went through a hole in the straw and into the mud.

One of the pips germinated. It sent up its first little leaves, then more, and began to form a twig, and then a little stem.

And in about fifteen years more there was a respectable tree. And in twenty quite a well-grown one.

Boys would come for the apples and get a particularly bad stomach-ache from them.

After thirty years there was a well-set tree, standing by itself and being a well-known landmark. A boy climbed it one year to watch the Boat Race, fell out, and broke his arm.

It was not a very kindly tree. It dropped a branch on little Jenny Nokes and scratched her face for ever.

"It didn't mean to," she said. "It raised its hat ever so politely."

But they all said she was concussed too, and gave her soothing medicine.

And one year, when the tree itself should have been in its prime, when it was indeed full of leaves and the fruit was ripening, every leaf one night turned yellow, and the apples began to fall, and worms to crawl from them.

A man and his young son were walking along the riverside at that moment. The sound of tumbling apples made the boy look. He saw them falling, and he saw the leaves curling and the twigs moving like hands, the boughs flailing like arms, and the roots lifting like legs.

Out of the top of the tree fell a hat.

"Why," said the man, picking it up, "it's just like the hat I brought back one year, when your uncle was just a young man, and he told me some tale and threw it in the river. A very larky man in those days, your uncle Edwin."

Edwin was now the Bishop of Faraway.

The father was Gordon, now rich and settled.

But the imp, or elf, in the hat had been waiting for him all the same.

The tree picked him up and ate him, body and mind and soul and all.

The boy went home, brought an axe, chopped the tree down and threw it back in the river. The imp got back to China in the end.

∽ℋorsehair ∽

Martinhall's Brewery is still in the City of London. The barges with grain come up to King John's wharf, and always will because the brewery has a right to that for ever, signed by King John himself. You can see it at the office any Thursday, from two to four in the afternoon.

The Brewery land was given to Sebastian Martinhall by Edward the Fourth in 1465 because his sister was so pretty. They don't pay any rates or taxes.

They grow their own barley in fields leased to them by Oliver Cromwell, and they malt it in the city. They buy hops from the Archbishop of Canterbury's estates near Westerham in Kent.

They keep their horses at the Brewery. Queen Elizabeth the First granted them that right for ever. The horses eat hay from a Royal Estate in Wales, where it is all cut by hand. The horses go there for a holiday each year, and talk about it all the rest of the time.

You'd think with all this they couldn't go wrong. But they did, just a bit, a year or two ago. Because all this happy good luck depends on making good beer all the time. Start making bad beer and it all closes down, all the grand people won't allow bad beer to come out. And they haven't to throw away a drop, but drink or sell the lot. So there's no hiding what they do.

So what went wrong was tinned lager. Everybody wanted cans of lager. That's what we want, the innkeepers say, the ones who keep those little bars, the folk buying to take a drink home or to the football. Four-packs, six-packs, eight-packs, twenty-four-packs, you name it, there's a ring-pull.

Martinhall's made a lager. They made it for five years in small lots until they got it right. They put it in cans. They spent two years researching cans. They spent a year designing them. They spent six months advertising.

Then they loaded their wagons with it and sent it out. The horses found the load was the same, just the noise different.

And it was a success. It was a wow. It was terrific. It was the best lager in the world. It was wanted by the cartload. It was wanted by the tanker.

Until then only the City folk really knew about Martinhall's. But now the world began to know. It was good for the firm. Mr Martinhall got a new car. He went in it to the Palace and they drank, well, you name it, there wasn't anything else they could drink that year, was there?

The staff asked for new uniforms. They wanted to be known. They were proud of the best lager in the world.

But in an old establishment, that has never moved or even built a new building since the time of Henry the Eighth's third wife, there are employees who don't want anything to change.

Mr Martinhall grew very proud of the turnout of the horses, and the drivers had new livery. The horses shone in particular, with their manes and tails brushed and combed and plaited as if they were made in a factory.

Mr Martinhall lived at the brewery with his wife, two sons, and three daughters. They went to school first thing each morning on the first dray out. Mr Martinhall noticed that day that the three daughters had their long hair brushed and combed and plaited as smart as the horses. He thought someone had been putting in some work, and he was proud of them too.

He didn't know who had put in the work. In the afternoon the daughters came home unhappy, and the sons had clearly been in fights. They had one and all had a bad day in school, their lessons going wrong, their friends unkind, their enemies very beastly, and something foolish had happened to each one, like blots in books or dinner on the floor or an elbow in someone's eye.

Then the draymen came to the door with tales of woe of not being able to get up Ludgate Hill, or through St Swithin's Lane, of the horses bewitched it seems and wouldn't back up or drive straight, of the cartons of lager

falling off under buses and being crushed, of getting parking tickets or threated with being towed away, and a sad day for all, nothing delivered; of the new lager tanker being broken down on the M1.

The draymen off-loaded all their beer and lager, and settled the horses down for the night, brushed out their tails and their manes and groomed them. But the horses weren't happy, they said. They were shaking their heads and stamping and biting their hayracks, and something was wrong.

Mr Martinhall thought it had never happened before, so it would never happen again. But the telephone rang all evening, publicans wondering where their supplies were, and it's all very well, Mr Martinhall, but what about tomorrow?

Mr Martinhall opened himself a can of lager and drank it. It tasted as well as ever. There was nothing wrong with that. But something was wrong.

In the morning everything looked perfect again. The horses were bright and ready and smart as could be, not a hair out of place.

The children were as neat as ninepence, the girls' little school hats perched on their braids, only the boys complaining they had knots in their hair like dried jam.

Just, they didn't want to go to school. And the horses took a look at the street outside and decided they were frightened of the traffic they really knew perfectly well.

Well, said Mr Martinhall, we'll declare the day a holiday, that's fair. So the horses went back in their stables, the children to their rooms, and the draymen off home. The bottling stopped in the brewery, the malting in the ovens, and the fermenting in the vats. A holiday is a holiday.

Mr Martinhall sat in his quiet office. He wandered in the quiet brewery. He looked over the Thames from the still wharf where barley was loaded. He went down to the stables and talked to the horses. Some of them had been working when he was a drayman learning the whole brewing trade.

They blew into his ear, but he did not know the words. He looked at the plaits in the manes and tails. He went up to his office, and into the room beyond, where they kept the signature of King John and the thumbprint of the Archbishop and the seal of Oliver Cromwell.

There he looked in ancient books to see whether anybody from old times knew what was going on.

He found a very old parchment, signed by Ethelred the Unready, in Anglo-Saxon writing rather unsteady, saying that the proprietors of the land had to be consulted (*gewitan hæf*) by candlelight (*candel lieg*) before changes were made to the beer (*wallop*).

But, thought Mr Martinhall, surely I am the proprietor, being given the land by Edward the Fourth in 1465? And had he not consulted himself before any changes, and hadn't there been none, for lager is made of exactly the same stuff as beer, very nearly?

In the very dark of the night he got from his bed and went down into the deep cellars, beyond the stables, with a candle. This was the only place he had not looked. He sat down on an upturned bucket and waited to see what happened.

By and by a little man came up to him with a jug of beer and a cannikin, and they shared the beer. It was Martinhall's best, in perfect condition.

"You've got it wrong, Martinhall," said the little man. "I've been here since the Saxons and this is the first time Martinhall's has made that nasty light stuff, and it has to stop."

"Nobody tasted better lager, they say," said Mr Martinhall.

But the little man said, "My folk sent me out to tell you to make no more. We don't like it. It swells our bellies. I can't stop them plaiting the hair of the horses, and when they do that the horses won't go very well; and they plaited the hair of your children, and they did not do so well. You never consulted us, and we say, no more lager."

"But," said Mr Martinhall, "we have to sell all our beer or lose the shop."

Then the little man laughed. "That's not beer in those cans," he said, "so pour it down the river."

In the morning the lager vat was dry, all the cans were crushed, and the horses were rare and ready with plain tails and manes to deliver casks of true beer. The daughters were ready for school, and the sons merely tidy.

And Martinhall's lager you very likely won't have tasted – which is lucky because it would spoil all other lagers for you – and what's more you never will. It is no longer brewed.

Mr Martinhall keeps a candle on his desk, in case there is another mistake. He'll tell you why, Thursday afternoons between two and four.

☜ℋey Diddle Dinkety ☞

Hey diddle dinkety, poppety, pet,
   The merchants of London they wear scarlet;
Silk in the collar and gold in the hem,
   So merrily march the merchant men.

❦ The Old Cow ❦

There was a farmer who lived Richmond way, ploughed a few fields by the river, and kept one cow for the milk. One day he was leaning on the gate, looking at the cow. She was now too old to give milk, and too thin to sell. The farmer was wondering what to do about it, because he had a wife and several children who were getting rather thin too, and becoming critical of him. The cow never complained.

Then, just as Richmond clock struck two, a stranger came and leaned on the gate beside him.

"I am looking for a beast to buy," said the stranger.

"You should go to Richmond market in two days' time," said the farmer. "Or Twickenham on Mondays, if you can trust them. Or perhaps," he said, "you would like to buy this one? I do not think she would be a good bargain, but that is up to you."

The stranger looked at the cow. "No," he said, "my people would never buy that cow. She needs a great deal of improvement."

"She has a gentle nature," said the farmer. "Never puts her foot in the pail. Never talks back. If you want that sort of thing the house is full of smart children."

"I am obliged to you for your kindly response," said the

stranger. "All the same, I must be on my way." And off he went, quite quickly, the farmer thought, and lucky not to trip over in the rough road. But he moved very lightly.

The farmer went in to tell his wife. She was not pleased. "Surely you could have come to some arrangement," she said. "I must have married you for your good looks, not your good sense." And the little children stared at him, because they were hungry.

So the farmer went out of the house again, leaned on the gate again, and looked at the cow again.

In a little while he heard people approaching. They came along the road talking and laughing, and full of high spirits. They were calling out for someone as they came, and getting no reply. "Where is he?" they asked each other.

Then, all at once, they saw the farmer, and came crowding up to him. "Where have you been?" they said. "We have been searching for you."

"I have been leaning on this gate," said the farmer.

"Well, come along," said the people. "We are all hungry by now. Is that the only beast you could buy for us?"

Now, the farmer was a little surprised by all this, but he had been keeping his eyes open, and could tell by the way these people walked that they were not ordinary mortals like himself, and came from further off than Richmond –

Twickenham perhaps (which isn't a good sign) or even Hampton Wick. Then he saw that their feet did not touch the ground, and decided they were the fairies, on some jaunt, come out of the country for the day.

I must not lose this opportunity, he thought. They mistake me for the stranger who would not buy the cow. But they think they have bought it. And no doubt that the owner has been paid.

"This is the beast," he said. "But we should pay the farmer first."

"We shall pay him," said the leader of the travellers. "The farmer will trust the fairies, of course. So come along with it."

"I knew I was right," said the farmer, and opened the gate and drove the cow along. He followed last, because his feet touched the ground like a man's, and the cow's were heavier still.

They went down by the river, where the grass was long and green. There they roasted the old cow, and ate her quite up.

They will never pay me, thought the farmer. She is too tough. And he could not bear to eat her himself.

But there was a great deal more than old cow to eat. The fairies had brought all their own foods of honey and milk and cakes of white flour. The farmer ate all of that he could, and then filled his pockets with fine breads, delicious cake, and marvellous fruit, to take home and please his family – indeed to feed them at all.

All the afternoon he sat by the riverside and watched the fairies at play. They could pull down lightning and turn it into crowns; or take a tree and make it into any wooden thing and put it back as a tree, still growing; they could touch the ground and fountains would spring up; they could play with lions as children play with kittens.

They would not let him go. "Stay," they would say, and he could not rise up and walk. So he closed his eyes, and snored a little, and the fairies said, "He has been too long in the earth, and is full of man's need to sleep."

As dusk came, the fairies made ready to go back to the countryside where the sun never sets. "We must be away now," they called. "We must find home again."

The farmer got up and said, "What about paying for the cow you bought from the farmer?"

"Tonight," said the fairies. "We shall send it tonight. Do not trouble yourself about it. The farmer will be happy."

Alas, thought the farmer, the fairies have days that are longer than the world. I shall never get my money.

Then the troop of fairies left. The farmer tried to follow them and keep up. At first that was easy, because they walked just above the ground at running pace. Then they flew higher, even without wings.

The farmer clung to the clothes of two of them as they went by. But when he was as high as a tree he felt heavy; when he was as high as a bird he grew weary; when he was at the clouds he fell down, and down.

The fairies did not notice. The farmer came head over heels all the way and landed in his own backyard, in his own midden, and sat there dazed, and somewhat bruised.

His wife came out of the house to throw soapsuds on the midden, and saw him sprawling in the sweepings from the byre.

"What are you doing?" she said. "Are you trying to

improve what beauty you have? Or are you thinking? Or have you hidden gold in the midden?"

"It is none of those things," said the farmer. "I have been with the fairies, and sold them the cow, and I have been at the feast and brought away some fine food. I would have flown away with the fairies, but I wished to return to you."

"Let us have no more of this nonsense," said his wife. And the children gazed at him and blinked slowly. It is foolishness having children at all, and they are not slow to remind you.

"But look," said the farmer, and began to turn out his pockets to show the fine bread from the feast, and the sweet fruits.

But all he could find was a little hay, and dried leaves, and the fruit had turned to little pebbles.

"You should come to your senses," said his wife. She threw the soapsuds on him, and the children shook their heads and went indoors. They knew.

The farmer went sadly off to lean on the gate again. When he was doing so something came and stood beside him.

He thought it was a stranger again, or the fairies returning, and would not look. There was trouble that way, he knew. He took no notice, while Richmond clock struck ten.

And at the last stroke something licked his ear. It was no stranger, but his own cow. She was no longer old and thin, but plump, and ready to be milked. And it was obvious no one had eaten her.

"The fairies have paid," said the farmer to his wife, taking a pail of milk into the house. She and the children were amazed, and happy again.

But the fairies have never again mistaken the Richmond farmer for one of themselves.

⚭ *The Milestoner* ⚭

They digged something up out the chalk in the Kent Road, the Old Kent Road they call that now, long and ago before the New One. On about the fifth milestone out. Yes, the fifth, they say, five miles to London, seventy-five to Dover, top of the hill.

Digged it up when they was getting flintses for facing London Tower. That come out and looked at them and they got away out quick bar the last one and he come out dead. That throwed um out after.

They never got no flintses more out of that hole. Never went near. Only lads, and fools like that, would go and listen to the hole, and there was that inside, talking and snoring to its ownself.

And the biggest fool would drop a lump of chalk in and wait. And the chalk would come out again, and what was inside would shout a bit that he couldn't eat chalk. And the lads would think it the freshest joke ever, and just run one mile home, or maybe seventy-five to Dover; all fools.

It had to be chalk, mind, for if they bowled in a lump of flint, then that inside would sing and shout for more. If the lads went close they heard that old flint being split and crushed, like it was the kernel of a nut, cracked and grinded.

And if they stayed close then out would come something like a long bristly arm, and sweep about the place to catch what it could. Once it catched a boy, and drew him right in the hole, and throwed him out again, and he wasn't dead at all, but by no means any good after, they saw. But most folk never seen him before, so there's no telling.

Of course, they never saw what snored or shouted or came out, because they went in the dark. But when they were idle again they'd go and tease at the hole again.

Then, after a time, it wasn't there. They don't know how long the time was, but it was grandfathers who remembered hearing that thing, and grandsons couldn't find the spot.

So they thought the hole was all fallen in and if it was buried it was dead, and by the time these grandsons was grandfathers themselves it was just a tale, just a remembrance of something in that place. But now folk would walk past and just lip out the words of a prayer, and all would be well.

Just to say uneasy, they said. Not a spot to linger in – there's been deeds there, and like if something watched and waited by the milestone, five miles from London Tower.

Lurked, they thought, as time went on. Something lurked behind the milestone. In the shadow. Where the chalk lies white and nothing grows.

But of course if you hear of a thing you expect it.

One day a stranger came through, not just out of Dover, but from beyond the seas, and up the hill he went at dusk. At the top is the milestone, and that filled-up pit behind, and no one said ought; no one felt need to, just an old tale, and not knowing the man's words for anything.

That traveller came back down the hill quite stark mad; and worse for talking a strange language. But parson heard and came. Got to get the nonsense out of local heads, he said, and got into Latin with the traveller. Started off sharp, and then slowed, then shook his head and went through slower and slower, bound to believe what he heard. And told folk in plain English what it was.

Top of the hill, it seems, fellow come out from the back of the milestone, talking fair, far as parson could tell from the foreign gentleman. Not threatening, just asking if he could walk along aways with the traveller, not knowing the road, but wanting to be in London Town before the gates closed. Business in there, he said.

Then all the moon come up like a fire, and the chalk all white, and that from back of the milestone come clear as day. And then the parson say that Latin got no words to tell what that thing was like, except it wasn't one mouth with teeth, but many, and they grinded and they grinded. And it jumped on the traveller's back, to be carried on its way. It got no proper legs, more like a lobster-style of thing, crawling and not walking, but able to cling.

They took the poor foreign gentleman into his own country again and we never heard of him more.

And some went up other nights to see what the Latin hadn't go no words for, but they saw nothing.

Then in a bit there came a lady in her coach, coachman, footman, her baggage and her little boy, hasty in the village, to be on their way before the gates closed at the city wall.

They never got there. There was just the screaming of them, up on the hill, before you could have sung a psalm.

And in the morning there was the carriage burst apart, the little boy dead with terror, his mother staring blind, said she would never look again on this world. The servants not about, but stole nothing. The constable heard they came to the city gates when they were closed and ran on and round the city and never heard of again, but might be the ones taken up mad in Rochester next day and died in Bedlam.

The lady died too. She said she saw that thing, but her tongue hadn't words for it either, so that's Latin and English. It wanted a ride, and . . . but then she lost her soul.

There were more, one sort and another. They talked about a new road, but not for a hundred years. And the folk nothing in any way grand, so no one recalls them.

Then there came a poor traveller, blind as a stone, touching the road with his stick and getting on steady. Got to get on, he said, be in the city gate. And so he would go.

This is the tale as it must be. He got up to the milestone, and that thing come forward and accosts him for company, same as many a time. But on this occasion the blind fellow don't see anything of him, no mouths filled with teeth, or body like a lobster or great fly. He must have been frightened, but what's he to do, a poor man and a blind man, but take him along?

So that thing gets up on his back, and off they go, stick tapping, the thing grinding its teeths, and talking.

So they go through the villages, and then in the suburbs,

and to the bridge, and the city gate beyond, and it's dark by
then.

Just, what do you carry? says the guard, not bothering,
off duty next minute when they close up the gate. And
taking no notice of what the old blind fellow said. Just off to
the Tower, my friend here been a long time owed his dues,
all those flint stones been stolen from his larder, and he's a-
come for them.

Well, they go on. But the guard tell his tale, and the
constable thinks he'll follow, for stones in the Tower might
be the jewels on the crowns and these days nothing sacred.
So he followed, sure enough along the way to the Tower,
past the fish market, and bottom of the hill he catched up
and enquired.

That's it, said the blind man. To the Tower, he said, and
get the man's stones back, and the constable saying, see
here, you can't do that, and the blind man saying, yes, he'll
get along Tower Pier, that's the best way, constable, I know
the streets, and my friend here doesn't know one inch of
them, so along Tower Pier, direct me.

The constable begins to think this is more Latin than
English, and the meaning is plain one way and another, and
the blind man is no fool, and maybe the bravest man he ever
met.

So he said he would go in front, and there he went, and
put the blind man on the pier.

Is it straight on? the blind one wants to know, and it is,
says the constable, and stands aside. Then he follows, and
then he says, good evening, gentlemen.

Because at the end of the pier the blind man swishes with
his stick to know where he is, and walks straight on, and

down into the water.

And when they pull him out they think a dreadful monster fish caught him, and then drownded with him, but first it chewed off his head. And the blind man was out of the way brave, but no one knew who he was. Only that he paid for his beer with a bad shilling, and for his duty with his life.

And at the top of the hill by the milestone there's nothing awkward at all, just a tidy little bungalow some old folks live in.

At the Tower nothing came to eat the flintses out of that thing's larder. And there's a new Kent Road, and there's railways, and I shouldn't wonder one day if they fly to Dover in two minutes.

↬ *The Wales House Ghost* ↫

Wales House was the big house in Finchley, designed by Sir Christopher Robin or one of those, then added to by Sir Gilbert Memorial a long time ago. The house isn't there now at all and they don't know where it used to be, even its post code being lost. Nothing happened to it, like keeping it in repair, so it fell away and dropped down and got rubbled, bits of it carted off to fill holes and build motorways and rabbit hutches.

Mr Makredo lived there. He married into it, so his wife was Lady Jane. The Mister was rich, now he had Lady Jane and the house, and he was rich before. He had a coach, and would go in it to London and take his supper, do business and gambling about, and come home with gold and jewels, but where he put this stuff he never told Lady Jane, and a lad called Peterkin was his coachman, and he never saw or heard a word. But he knew there was a black bag, coming heavy and going light.

"Back tonight," the Mister would say to Lady Jane.

"Where shall you be?" she would ask.

"On the road home," the Mister would say, and dab her a kiss, and wink at the baby, and off he went.

And one night he came back, and when Peterkin got the

coach door open for him the Mister sat there with never a word. He had leaned back and died after his big dinner in the City, and all his work.

So Lady Jane came out and fetched in the black bag, only this time it came back light, and Peterkin lifted out the Mister, stiff as a chair.

There was a funeral, and the Mister was put in the family vault just over the churchyard wall. It was Lady Jane's family, not the Makredos', but he was family now.

Lady Jane looked in the light bag and found not much. "I can live here," she said to Peterkin, "but not keep coach and horses, but you can be all the other servant-men, or leave and do better."

She sold the horses and coach, and Peterkin stayed about and worked the garden and fetched the coals, and it might have been worse for both of them.

But when a few weeks had gone by, the Mister seemed to get up from his burial place. Lady Jane saw him about the house.

"It's my fancy," she told Peterkin.

"Yes, my Lady," said Peterkin.

"Rattling in the kitchen stove," said Lady Jane. "Drumming in the chimney; and the carpet goes hump-a-wump under my feet."

And of course Peterkin had no carpet out in the stable where he lived, and no horses to keep him warmed. "Yes, my Lady," he said.

In a month the Mister was still there, and worse.

"He comes into my room," said Lady Jane. "He makes faces at the baby. He broke the wardrobe."

"Yes, my Lady," said Peterkin. But he thought it was the baby did that, but not his place to say so. They would tell him he didn't know babies.

One night Lady Jane had enough of that. She came running out over the cobbles to the stable at midnight or two in the morning, no right to be awake, and fetched Peterkin out of his loft, and brought him into the house.

"He's in here," she told him. "Mr Makredo. Up and down the stairs, breaking the jam in the jars, playing on his violin." The Mister had been good on the violin.

"Maybe he wants it with him in the vault," said Peterkin. "Come back for it, like."

"And he tipped over my bed," said Lady Jane. "See."

But Peterkin would not go further than the landing. He would be frightened of the baby, that was it. But he was not frightened of the Mister, even if he was a ghost. If you get to carry the corpse about, set hard like a chair, you give nothing for the spirit after.

"I'll bide here," he said. "I'll have a word if I can. If not, I'll say nothing."

It turned out he said nothing, because the ghost of the Mister did not stop to pass the time of night. He just passed Peterkin twice or thrice, on his way to break a window or to stand by Lady Jane's door and wring his hands, because he never meant to break the window, Peterkin thought, but did the wrong action and couldn't help himself. At last he sank through the floor, not looking where he was going.

In the morning Lady Jane boiled Peterkin an egg, and said, "What do you think it is, Peterkin? Why does he bother me so and alarm my baby daughter?"

"He hasn't learnt to be dead," said Peterkin. "It doesn't come all at once. It's a skill. He hasn't anyone to tell him how to behave."

"We must get the parson," said Lady Jane.

"It would be best," said Peterkin. But he did not mean what Lady Jane meant.

"To get him buried better?" she asked.

"No, not that," said Peterkin.

"The other thing is weddings," said Lady Jane. "Do you mean that, Peterkin?"

"No, my Lady," said Peterkin. "That is not my station in life. We want him for something else."

"But if you change your mind," said Lady Jane, "well, that is still a matter for the parson. That is two thoughts. What is the third."

"Why," said Peterkin, "to bury me in the family vault."

"Oh dear," said Lady Jane. "In the vault?"

"I have been in your service all my days," said Peterkin. "I am as good as family, and paid less."

"And is being dead and buried better than taking me?" asked Lady Jane

"Now, listen, my Lady," said Peterkin. And he told her what he had in mind, and what his plan was.

She listened and she did it. She had Peterkin declared dead and laid out in the stable. She came to look at him, and the baby laughed, and Peterkin asked for a cup of tea. "And on no account screw down the coffin lid," he said. "Or you've buried me proper."

"You are such a kind boy," said Lady Jane.

Next day they had the funeral; the church bell rang, the sexton led the prayers, the parson turned the key in the vault, and that was Peterkin put tidy away.

"He was a very good and faithful servant," said Lady Jane. "The baby liked him, and he brought in firewood."

Because of what he had told her she was not surprised at what he did next time they met, though she was a little cross later.

Before that, though, it was night-time in the vault, and indeed all over Finchley and its farms and fields and little River Brent.

In the night-time the Mister stepped right out of his coffin. Just as he did so Peterkin tipped off his coffin lid and stepped out with him.

"Now then," said the Mister. "Who's that?"

"Oh," said Peterkin, all slow and sad, "it's me, Peterkin, died yesterday and I don't know a thing about it except I felt strange; and I was just buried today and it's thin bedcovers they gave me and I'm cold."

"That's how it is," said the Mister. "Come along with me. There's something I have to do."

"What is it?" asked Peterkin.

"I don't remember until I get there," said the Mister. "Then it's too late to tell. Maybe the two of us can work it out."

And with that he was through the vault door and in the churchyard, and then through the wall and in the garden of Wales House.

"Wait for me," said Peterkin. "I'm just dead a minute, and I haven't got hold of the right way to do things yet."

The ghost of the Mister came back and unlocked the vault door. "You have a lot to learn," he said. "And that bit's easy. But I just can't quite get in my mind what I do the rest of the time. It's like I don't care about something I once cared for a lot, and it goes out of my mind."

"The baby, perhaps," said Peterkin.

"There's one in the back of the vault," said the Mister, "got a lot to say for itself and been doing so this last hundred years. Not great learners at that age. Now we'll just go through the churchyard wall."

But Peterkin had to haunt through the churchyard gate. "Just used to horses," he said. "Not broken in to this caper yet."

"Come on," said the Mister. "In the house now, something to do in the house."

But he couldn't recall what it was.

They went into the house, and the Mister turned the door handles and let them go so that they whirred. He pulled at the cat's tail. He went through the wall into Lady Jane's bedroom, and Peterkin had to call him back to open the door.

"My hand goes through the knob," said Peterkin, making it all up. "Like trying to catch a shadow."

"What's a shadow?" said the Mister. He didn't have one any more. "You're still talking like a live person."

"I've not been at it long," said Peterkin, following the Mister into Lady Jane's bedroom.

Peterkin felt uncomfortable there, because she sat up in bed looking cross and frightened while the Mister knocked about the stuff on the dressing-table and tried to set the cradle swinging.

Peterkin did what the Mister did, and broke a candlestick. He had said he would have to do what the ghost did, but he would only break a few small things.

Lady Jane, watching them both, thought they were both ghosts. Then the ghost frightened the baby, and Peterkin rocked it to sleep.

"I can learn it from you," said the Mister.

"It's your baby," said Peterkin.

"How did I manage that?" said the Mister. "I've been dead for weeks."

They haunted the bedroom. They haunted the landing. They went to haunt the kitchen.

"What's that door?" said the Mister, suddenly.

"It's the cellar," said Peterkin. "There's nothing down there. The Mister always kept its floor clear."

"Who was he?" said the ghost. "What Mister?"

"Mr Makredo," said Peterkin.

"Never heard of him," said the ghost. Of course Mr Makredo was the ghost, but Peterkin began to wonder, and hope being dead wasn't infectious.

"Do you want to be down in the cellar?" he asked the Mister. Peterkin knew where the key was.

"I've got a very good vault," said the Mister. "What do I want with a cellar?"

"We'll go back then," said Peterkin. He thought he might have to stay another night or two in the vault before he found out what was going on. But he wasn't in the greatest hurry, because Lady Jane had done as he asked and left him a slice of pie and a mug of milk, and he was eating those.

"I don't understand what you are doing," said the Mister.

"I'm just new dead," said Peterkin. "I don't know how to

say all the words, so I'm just putting a few in my mouth
ready for later on. Do you want to try them?"

The ghost of the Mister enjoyed some crust and a sip of
the milk. "What have I eaten?" he asked.

"It might be the words for Heaven," said Peterkin. "It
might be the words for Hell."

"Enough of all that," said the Mister. "Did we go down the
cellar?"

"You take a look," said Peterkin. "I'm just finishing off the
jelly round the meat." It was a long time since he died, and
of course he never got invited to his funeral tea.

So the Mister went down into the cellar, and Peterkin
thought he should follow, not knowing what the ghost
might forget, or remember, and not wanting to find the
Mister had gone home without him. Peterkin could not
bear the thought of going into the vault
alone, only with company.

So he took the candle into the
cellar. And there he saw the
Mister kneeling down.

"Too late for prayers," said
Peterkin.

"I left something down here,"
said the Mister, scratching
away at the floor. "I keep
trying to tell her, but I can't
carry it in my head all the way
up the stairs. See."

And where he scratched Peterkin saw a loose stone, and
when the Mister scratched in another place there was
another, and the same in a third place.

"Well," said the Mister, "I'm wakeful now, so it's time to go to bed."

"Well, so it is," said Peterkin, having a better scratch at the third place and finding a jar of copper coins.

"I wish I remembered why I walk," said the Mister.

"It's something to wonder about," said Peterkin, scratching at the second place and finding a jar of silver coins.

"It's so restless," said the Mister. "I should be dreaming like a good body."

"Well, you do that," said Peterkin, finding a third jar full to the top with gold coins. "Good-day to you."

"Good-day to you," said the ghost. "Don't dream of living people, because that's a daymare."

So off the Mister went. Peterkin stayed in the cellar longer. Then he went upstairs to the kitchen and put the fire on to burn, and did what he had to do.

In the morning Lady Jane came down and Peter had gone to his own bed. Lady Jane set to making bread, and put it to rise beside the baby before the fire.

Then Peterkin came in, hoping for breakfast.

"I don't know," said Lady Jane. "You broke a candlestick. And what's to happen tonight? The chamber pot?" And by now she was pummelling a loaf ready for baking, so Peterkin got himself a pot of tea, or perhaps it was ale. There's no one to ask.

All the time Lady Jane was scolding him, knocking up a second loaf. She thought there was some trick up his sleeve, and besides she thought he smelled of the vault and that one day she will too. And she held the third loaf down until it squealed.

But in the end she put the bread in the oven to bake, and went off with the baby and the hourglass.

"Be out of my kitchen before I come back," she told Peterkin. "You've done no good."

And when she had gone Peterkin did what he had to do and went to wait inside the cellar door.

Lady Jane came back when the glass ran out, and went to get the three loaves from the oven.

She didn't look to see what she was doing until she had them all on the table. Then, at the top of her voice she called for Peterkin.

"I'm in trouble," said Peterkin, coming out of the cellar.

"You are the greatest fool," said Lady Jane.

Because, you know, what she got from the oven was not three loaves, but a jar of copper, a jar of silver, and a jar of gold.

"The Mister could not remember what he meant to tell you," said Peterkin, "that it was down in the cellar. It's the way with ghosts. I told you he had something to learn in that trade."

"You hold the baby while I count this," said Lady Jane.

And how it was, Peterkin held the baby to this day, or as long as he lived, baby, little girl, big girl, young woman, mother, grandmother, and then he lost count. Lady Jane thought she'd best remember the Mister and give other fellows the go-by.

Of course, if Peterkin had waited another night the Mister would have shown him three more jars of pearls and jewels and spoons, but they're still there under Wales House, and you've only to look to find them.

∽ *In The Bleak Midwinter* ∽

The boy will have to go for it," said Hugo's father. "I cannot go – I have to be about my work. Why should he sit by the fire when there is work to be done? I work each day of the year, Christmas or not. He must do his share."

Hugo's father was kennel-keeper to the huntsmen of Bromley. He had to walk four hounds back there from Southend at once, through open country, fields and woods and flint walls, and miles from London. London has now walked nearer and nearer and swallowed all those places.

"What do you need me for?" asked Hugo. He wanted to be useful to his mother and father, which is difficult for a dreamer. He did not wish to be in the wintry fields watching animals, or be shouted at for spilling the afternoon's milk. He had, as usual, not been listening, only looking forward to getting a present the next day, Christmas Day.

"Go to your grandmother's house," said his mother. "You know exactly where it is, by Ladywell just beyond Catford. It is only a mile or two away. Bring back my little cloth bag of saffron. It went there at harvest time, and it has not come back because we have not visited since."

Hugo was thinking he was comfortable by the fire as he was, just getting warm from fetching water from the spring, and not caring about saffron, not even knowing what it was.

"No, do not look stupid," his mother went on. "I must bake the bread for Christmas Day, and it has to be golden with saffron, and here there is no saffron. Hurry there and back, and do not sit by her fire. Also, do not fall into Catford Brook."

So Hugo had to stand up and set off. It was two miles to the next village. He met no one in the fields. When he climbed the stile at each flint and stone wall there was only the faded grass beyond in the next field.

The wind climbed the stiles with him, nipping at his heels, like a dog. But there were no real animals, and it was too cold even for an imaginary dog. The wind was from somewhere in the north and brought with it the reek of London. The air was too cold for Hugo to linger in it and dream.

"I shall not be in trouble for that," he thought, walking quickly to keep warm.

At Ladywell his grandmother said, "Well, do not stand in my doorway," when she had heard what he wanted. "No, do not come in either. Be on your way before it is dark."

She gave him the little screw of saffron in its cloth, holding it between finger and thumb. Hugo held it between his finger and thumb, and it weighed, oh, nothing. He could smell its warm smell. Saffron is smell and flavour and colour. His grandmother opened the packet and showed him the costly red threads.

"This is a precious spice, so do not lose it," she said. She pushed the tiny package into his pocket, folded down the pocket flap, and sent him on his way. "Bring me some of the bread tomorrow," she said. "It is all the Christmas gift I need."

She closed the door, and went back to her work. She was a laundress at a palace near by. Hugo stamped his feet, patted his pocket, and set out for home. It was even colder now, and there were deep shadows in the sky.

He was alone. No person walked the same way, or met him. He wrapped his coat closely to him. A star came out and watched him.

Hugo saw it, and longed for a fine warm stable, with comfortable hay, where he could lie safe and sound and talk to the horses. That was because of the Christmas story and the star in the east. But it would be as comfortable to be lying with the hounds of Bromley hunt in their straw-filled kennel.

Under his feet the grass began to feel different. It was turning into white straw, stiff with frost. He heard his feet walking in it, and his ears began to sting with real cold.

Frost began to settle on the walls. First it made the edges sharp against the sky. Then it was like icy fur. The solitary star began to twinkle in it. There were sudden gleams of light like cold, cold fire.

All at once Hugo felt glad to be out in these fields, in the magical light and sparkle. It is like heaven, he thought, but no one will listen when I tell them. Why am I always shown what I cannot describe, things no one wants to know? He was suddenly out of a dream and into a special reality.

He thought nothing could be more beautiful, and that he

was the only one able to see it. However, to make certain everything was going right in the ordinary world he pulled the little pouch of cloth from his pocket, smelt the saffron, and put it back safely. Just me and it, out in the winter, he whispered to it. Both of us going home.

When he came to the next stile, and there were four more to go, something else began to happen. There had been many points of light along the tops of the walls, all cast out from the bright star above. But now the points of light were glowing inside the wall, between its stones, and with a warmer light than frost. Hugo knelt in the long grass and looked through a gap. He was sure something must be inside, among the stones. He thought that perhaps the cold was acting like iron, bringing sparks from the glassy flint.

The light inside was very different. Hugo had to blink several times to be sure he saw things right. The light was from little flames on tiny candles. The candles were being carried along by mice, each mouse clutching one in a claw, and getting along as well as it could on three legs, all hurrying in one direction.

There were mice going along alone. There were mice in families, holding the father's or the mother's tail. There were mice claw in claw. A very old bearded mouse was being carried by two strong young ones. As they went they talked to each other, excited, happy, busy.

The last of them went past the gap and there was darkness in that place in the wall. But when Hugo looked round he saw lights in other places as well, moving along, coming together where four walls met.

He had to find out what the mice were doing. He followed the light he had first seen. He watched again.

Mice were still going somewhere urgently. He heard them exchanging gossip, laughing, keeping their children in order. They knew what they were doing, where they were going, and were excited by it.

Overhead the sky grew dark, still with one star, but true night now. Inside the wall the crowd was bright and warm. Hugo longed to be their size and inside the wall with the crowd, holding a candle, part of the happiness. I would need a long tail, he thought.

The crowd had to slow down at last, because the mice were getting to their destination. The four walls joined here, like crossroads, and mice were coming along all these routes. Official mice began to tell others where to go.

They give orders even down there, thought Hugo. It is like my own life. But what are they about? Why are they here?

There was enough stone where the walls met to look like a building. Hugo had to clamber about, climbing up and along the wall until he saw what was going on.

Where the walls joined there was a hollow place inside, a room with a stone slab for a floor, tidy stone walls, and a stone slab for a roof. Hugo looked through a gap between flints very like a window.

Mice were crowding into this room. In it there was a little heap of neat mouse hay, and on it a bundle wrapped up. The crowd coming in stood back from this place. It seemed to be what they had come to visit. To one side of it sat a young mother mouse, to the other a father mouse. They were both shyly waiting to show the rest of the mouse world something.

The room filled with candlelight. Hundreds of mice sat waiting, growing quieter and quieter, more and more still. At last they were all ready.

Small mice came forward to help the mother mouse. Between them they lifted up the bundle on the hay and unwrapped it.

There was total silence. Then all the mice drew in their breaths with wonder, because they had seen nothing like this before. The mother mouse held up a baby mouse that was white all over, from its minute nose to the end of its little tail. The baby yawned sweetly, blinked so that all the mice sighed and Hugo's heart turned over and his eyes watered. Then the snow-white baby closed its eyes and fell asleep again.

And now another group came into the place. A grey mouse, a sandy mouse, and a black one made their way

through the crowd. Hugo saw crowns on their heads. They came forward and began to lay things in front of the baby mouse.

"It is Christmas, truly it is," said Hugo

to himself. "I know about it too. I know more than these mice. This is the first time for them, but I know what to do. But what can I give?"

There was only one thing for him to give, and he gave it. He opened the cloth pocket of saffron, laid it on the stone, pinched the contents up with his fingers, stretched his hand carefully and gently through the window, and laid the precious red threads in front of the baby white mouse.

The white mouse twitched its whiskers at him. No other mouse stirred. The gathering of mice knew his hand meant them no harm.

But in fact they went away all at once. It was like waking from a dream. Hugo found himself lost among the frozen fields, the only light coming from the single star. There were no candles, no mice. He could not find the hole in the wall. He knew that he had imagined what he saw.

"This is why I am useless to all the world," he said. "I cannot tell what is real. I am a very foolish boy."

He felt for the saffron, sure that he only imagined giving it away. "I shall not have to explain," he said.

But his pocket was empty, the little screw of cloth entirely gone. Only the faint smell of saffron still lingered, and when he breathed that up it too had gone.

He came home dreading what would happen. He hardly dared go into the house because of the trouble he would be in. But there is a time to stop dreaming, especially when frost is on all the fields. He opened the door and came into the firelight.

His mother was baking. She was kneading golden yellow bread. Hugo did not understand how she could be doing so without saffron, and he knew she had no saffron.

"You are a useless boy," she said, and Hugo knew there was great trouble.

"I know," he said. "I am sorry."

But his mother was not very cross. "You come in and leave the saffron and go out again," she said, "when I wanted you to fetch wood for me. You don't think. And as for my mother, I wonder where she kept my saffron. The bag smells as if it had been in a mouse's nest since harvest."

"But is it all right?" asked Hugo.

"It will do," said his mother. "Thank you for fetching it. Now sit by the fire. You must be cold."

Hugo sat, and could understand nothing.

Then, from the logs by his feet, a sandy mouse and a grey mouse and a black one scurried away along the wall and outside, their sharp eyes watching him. Hugo again thought they had crowns on their heads.

And then they had gone.

∽ *Pageant Silver* ∽

---

*The scene is a shabby yard in the city. No work is going on.
There are stacks of rubbishy wood. During the Chorus the
WIFE is searching her pockets and purse for a piece of money
she knows she has. In the distance a handbell is rung and
there is an indistinct announcement.*

*NATHANIEL HORNBEAM is looking at the rubbish
unhappily. TOWNSPEOPLE come in. BEGGAR is hobbling
on two sticks up through the audience.*

CHORUS: [Song, verse 1]:
> Within the ancient city's wall –
> We shall not say its name
> One far-off year the calendar
> To Corpus Christi came,
> The time when God proclaims his faith
> To man and wife and beast
> Who all come out on holiday
> Processions and a feast,
> From house and hall come one and all
> The greatest and the least.

TOWNSPEOPLE:

ONE: Each band of workmen,

TWO: [*interrupting*]: proud and technical

ONE: [*Continuing*]: must plan and build
THREE: A float
FOUR, THREE, TWO, ONE: A float!
NATHANIEL: [*sadly*]: A float!
TWO: to take about the town
THREE: and represent their guild.
FOUR: A prize is given for the best,
FIVE: the Master fines the worst,
ONE: A guild that does not show is driven from the town
ALL TOGETHER: accurst!
Some are pleased, but NATHANIEL is not. TOWNSPEOPLE
and NATHANIEL go out through archway. Enter BEGGAR.
He sees WIFE finding the coin at last and smiling on it.
BEGGAR: I bless you, lady, for your charity so kind. To
give Will surely bless us both and one of us will stay alive.
WIFE: It's all that is between my household and its supper
dish,
Enough to serve a crust, and skin and bone of river fish.
BEGGAR: If that's the case I'll leave this place, empty if
you wish.
They'll clear away my crumbling bones by early morning
light,
I'll feel no more the heat of day or chill of frosty night.
WIFE: No, take the coin, and fare you well; we'll find some
other meal.
Gives him the coin. The bell rings closer.
The GUILDMASTER enters after his BELLRINGER.
GUILDMASTER reads from scroll.
BEGGAR mumbles thanks, bows, hides from sight and goes
out, biting coin to test it.
GUILDMASTER: Nathaniel Hornbeam, navestock maker,

builder of the wheel.

NATHANIEL: Aye, that's my name, but as for trade, that's quite another tale.

I am the last of all my guild, but for my goods no sale
Has come my way for many a day.

GUILDMASTER: But now you must not fail.

The feast of Corpus Christi now is very close indeed;
Your guild must make a float for it.

NATHANIEL: But, Master, I must plead:

Excuse us from this burden, for we cannot bear the cost.
A silver coin is all we own . . .

WIFE: But that I fear is lost.

A man came by, about to die. To him the coin I tossed.

GUILDMASTER: It is a foolish thing your dame has done, Nathaniel.

The consequences of the act I do not need to tell.

A sorry, rough and shabby float will make the bishop frown;

But none at all will force the guilds to run you out of town.

He rings his bell and moves on, going off stage, and can be heard in the distance for a little while. NATHANIEL'S CHILDREN come on and run to their parents who are standing with arms hopelessly spread in their yard, looking at the rubbish.

GIRL: What troubles you, Mama, Papa? Why do you look so sad?

BOY: What bell was that, who rang it so, and is the meaning bad?

NATHANIEL & CHILDREN: [Song, verse 2]:

> Within the ancient city's wall –
> We shall not say its name

One far-off year the calendar
To Corpus Christi came,
The time when God proclaims his faith
To man and wife and beast
Who all come out on holiday
Processions and a feast,
From house and hall come one and all
The greatest and the least.

NATHANIEL
A trundle for a goose's eye,
A bridle for the cat;
A cage to keep the moonbeams in,
And what's the good of that?

BOY & GIRL: He has such fancies in his mind–
Nathaniel, do not rave.

NATHANIEL: We cannot build a pageant float
We'll leave – our lives we'll save.

BOY & GIRL: But we must try,
Disgrace defy –
Be cheeky and be brave!

BOY examines the clutter in the yard, pulling at a cart.
CREATURES run away, squeaking, and hide elsewhere.
WIFE and GIRL withdraw skirts and look disgusted.

BOY: The shafts are rotten and the floor has gone, but
with this cart,
See, something could be done, the wheels are good, and
that's a start.

NATHANIEL: I'll patch it up, but not for that. We'll make
our goods the load,
And when they come to turn us out we're ready for the
road;

With our disgrace upon our face, because we never
showed.

GIRL: Oh, Father dear, Mama and I will go indoors and cook.

NATHANIEL: Not even that. There was no change from
what a beggar took.

*NATHANIEL, WIFE, GIRL, BOY, go indoors. As night falls
little CREATURES come out of rubbish in the yard, and others
come on stage. They sit in a half- circle.*

BLACK RAT comes to the middle and speaks.

BLACK RAT: Members of the Minor Guild,
Are your bellies filled?

ONE: There's not a crumb
In my empty tum.

TWO: Hunger is all we've got;
We're cold, not hot.

THREE: What are we to do?
We could eat a shoe?

FOUR: Without any trouble
We could eat a shovel;

FIVE: And our palate
Would relish a mallet;

SIX: We could each digest
A packing chest.

BLACK RAT: We've starved before, and here we are, and
happy to complain.

But if the navestock maker has to leave and we remain,

In such events it is not sense to starve and starve again.

ONE: We have to help Nathaniel Hornbeam and his
pageant show.

TWO: We do not help him with his work then he is bound
to go.

THREE: We are so small,

FOUR: no help at all,

FIVE: and nothing useful know.

CREATURES: [Song, verse 3]:

> And people think we can't believe
> Because we are not men.
> They think we do not understand,
> But we can say Amen.
> We live and work beside mankind
> We share their ups and downs:
> And underneath their dwelling place
> We have our little towns;
> And if they grieve
> A sigh we heave,
> And tremble at their frowns.

BLACK RAT: We only hope that things come right if we indeed can't pray;

But for the moment we'll encourage them with loud hooray.

ALL CREATURES: Hooray, hooray.

NATHANIEL in his nightshirt comes out with a stick and shouts. A horn blows

NATHANIEL: Nightwatchmen come! Away, away.

CREATURES run off, 'Away, away' echoing 'Hooray, hooray'.

NIGHTWATCHMEN stamp in with lanterns.

NIGHTWATCHMEN [*Blows horn*]: A quiet night and all is well, and coming up to dawn.

NATHANIEL: I heard a noise. It was a snore, or something like a yawn.

NATHANIEL goes in again. NIGHTWATCHMEN cross stage and go out. They see BEGGAR close by and shout at him until he leaves across stage.

NIGHTWATCHMEN: Hey you, yes you, you vagabond, be off and please get lost.

No idlers here allowed, or into prison they'll be tossed.

NIGHTWATCHMEN go out. BOY and GIRL come on stage and start to look round yard and fetch out cart. They begin to cobble something together.

GIRL: There's rocks and twigs and rushes and a bucket with a leak.

BOY: We'll find us something splendid by the middle of the week.

GIRL: What can we do to show Our Lord in glory up on With rotten wood and clouts and on a cart that's sure to die?

BOY: We'll do our best. It is not very glorious, perhaps. And if we build it up too high it's certain to collapse.

GIRL: We need some help.

NATHANIEL enters and looks at what they are doing. He shakes his head

NATHANIEL [*Laughs bitterly*]: That's true enough. I think we'll pack our bags;

We've nought to eat and little left to keep us warm but rags [*He goes in again*].

BOY: Well, who will help us? All this work is hopeless. I'll give in.

I cannot finish such a job.

GIRL: How foolish to begin. [*Sobs slightly*]

BOY: Please do not cry. They'll think I've been unkind. I often am.

GIRL: But life's so often awful, happiness a painful sham.

BOY: We'll make the best of it and show the town our

bravest face.

A good attempt, however weak, is better than disgrace,
But none at all will mean we shall be driven from the
place.

BOY GIRL [Song, verse 4]:

BOY: How stupidly we started work
        How foolishly we tried;
        We could not find materials,
        And then my sister cried.

BOTH: Nathaniel is right, we fear
        We've wasted one whole day.

GIRL: From rubbish only rubbish comes
        A fine we'll have to pay.

BOTH: And in the murk
        The nettles lurk,
        And nothing goes our way

They begin to bundle osiers and reeds and assemble them on the cart.

GIRL: [*Sotto*] It is not very much like God in glory gone to heav'n.

BOY: Too dark to lay these bundles straight. They're all bound up unev'n.

The lights go down. BOY and GIRL go indoors. CREATURES enter and sniff and look at what has been done. They defer to BLACK RAT who comes in last.

BLACK RAT: How sad to see them poorer than ourselves. There's not much less
To own than what we haven't got. We'll do our best to bless
Their work, and tidy up. They are our share of humankind,

They may not ever think of us, but we have them in mind.
ONE: They do not think of us,
However much we fuss.
TWO: They don't know we exist –
We are not on their list.
THREE: And when we cheered
 He appeared
FOUR: He gave a great shout
And chucked us out.

One group has been looking at the cart and trying to make things better. They shake their heads and sit down glumly. Another group has been keeping watch and agitatedly sees something coming, and tries to attract BLACK RAT's attention.

BLACK RAT: There's little we can do to help, so onward must we plod
Our cheering did not help them, or our song go up to God.
It's no relief to lack belief, we must not think it odd.
FIVE: But Sir, another human
Is a-coming.
SIX: Poorer than the rest,
And raggedly dressed.

The BEGGAR enters. CREATURES stand aside respectfully, not afraid.

BEGGAR: I saw you come in here again. What is this gathering?
I know there's something that you need; last night I heard you sing.
BLACK RAT: Our squeaky little untrained voices in the treble clef:
Our noise was much too ugly, maybe heaven itself is deaf?

BEGGAR: It is not used to fervent prayers for anothers'
sake:
It was not deaf, but bored, and very likely not awake!
I am like you in poverty, but human I remain;
So I shall try a prayer now and hope it's not in vain.
BEGGAR [Song, verse 5]:
 When I was in a sorry plight
 Nathaniel's wife was kind;
 She gave me all her purse had held,
 And so that night I dined.
 I owe her life and soul and heart;
 Oh, could I heaven wake!
 Had I the pageant silver coin
 I'd give it back to make
 This very night
 The sky look bright
 With something for their sake!

*CREATURES group and join in as indicated. At end they go
out to one side, followed by BEGGAR, who looks back, and
shakes his head, because nothing has happened. After his exit,
when lights are low, there are snatches of song [the Carol] and
a small ANGEL comes on stage, looks about, then goes out
and comes back more bravely with companion.*

ANGEL 2: They've gone away. How sad. They did not
wait for our response.
The place is very hard to find
ANGEL 1: although we came at once.

Other angels enter. Recorders with snatches of Carol.

NATHANIEL [*Looks out*]: It is a dream. My supper was
too little to digest:
There's nothing worse than nothing much, and I can get

no rest. [*Goes in again*]

ANGEL 3: But morning comes, and men will be about. We must not show

Ourselves, but hurry with our work and quickly homeward go.

ANGEL 4: We'll touch and trim and glorify, repair and make and mend

To show how God came down to earth and will to heaven ascend

ANGEL 5: To demonstrate that charity is love and brings reward,

That heaven bends its ear at last when help has been implored.

ANGELS [Song, Verse 6]:

Man finds it hard to apprehend
We are not human sort
We measure out the charity,
By us good deeds are brought
To those who have been merciful;
To those whose life is hard
We bring triumphant messages
By act and deed and word,
For what will mend
Good faith will send
These children their reward.

ANGELS dance round the cart, touching it, but nothing seems to change. A bell rings. The ANGELS scurry about and go out. The bell rings again. The GUILDMASTER comes in.

GUILDMASTER: Assemble all your floats, the pageant will commence at once.

Be on your way and take your place among the day's
events
Do not delay, or stay away, this is your only chance.
NATHANIEL listens, then slams a window shut. GUILD-
MASTER moves on and into distance. BOY and GIRL come
out and look at cart.
BOY: We did our best with what we had, but nothing like
enough.
GIRL: Oh dear, by daylight in the town it's looking very
rough.
They go out with cart.   Off stage people begin to laugh.
Recorders play Song in transit to first station. NATHANIEL
comes on and shakes his head. WIFE joins him.
WIFE: The people jeer. They are so cruel, and they mock
the scene
Our children have prepared with twigs and rags and
rushes green.
NATHANIEL: Now they stand outside a merchant's house,
all on display.
There will be unkind words. He'll swiftly turn them both
away.
In the distance the Carol with drum, then recorders and
transit to new station, the stations being chosen for effect of
distant noise.
CAROL: Here we come gathering pity and alms,
Leading our pageant to show you its charms;
Answer our pleading and God bless your spouse,
Children and cattle, your fields and your house.
There is applause and cheering.
WIFE: He pitied them their sorry show. Let's hope it goes
as well

Elsewhere, that they bring back with them a happy tale to tell.

Carol at another station, and cheers, then transit to just offstage and Carol once again.

NATHANIEL: I do not understand. Our citizens are not so kind;

They do not show such mercy, we shall surely be fined.

ANGEL 1 enters pulling a rope. It is hard work. Others come on with their ropes.

WIFE: Oh, what is that? In all my days I never saw such things.

They look like long-lost children, yes, but why do they have wings?

The cart comes in. It is now a colourful and glorious float, with at least two stories, cherubs in the lower one, the BEGGAR arrayed in gold as God in glory at the top. The Carol is sung. The CREATURES all come in and stand shyly about.

BEGGAR: All creatures are from God.

BLACK RAT: What, even us, the scavengers?

CREATURES: And even thee and me and he, and other foreigners?

BEGGAR: Yes. Some are in his image, others sacred messengers.

You did not doubt yourselves, but asked how even you could pray,

The navestock maker's charity kept me alive to play

My part in this small taste of bliss, on Corpus Christi day.

VARIOUS: [Song, verse 7]:

GUILDMASTER: Nathaniel won the pageant prize
                  The navestock maker's skill
                  Has not deserted him.

WIFE: His wife
Did good as well as ill.
BOY & GIRL: We had a humble part to play
ANGELS: But all cannot be told.
NATHANIEL: Miraculous, mysterious,
The beggarman revealed;
TOGETHER: A manner wise
Just might disguise
The Maker of the World.
Enter all not on stage, WATCHMAN with horn, &c, &c
CHORUS [Song, verse 1, repeated]:
    Within the ancient city's wall –
    We shall not say its name
    One far-off year the calendar
    To Corpus Christi came,
    The time when God proclaims his faith
    To man and wife and beast
    Who all come out on holiday
    Processions and a feast,
    From house and hall
    Come one and all
    The greatest and the least.

CURTAIN

⤜ *Clinker at the Carney* ⤛

There was a rich maltster, the man who lets barley sprout and then cooks the sprouted grain and grinds it in his mill and sells it to the housewives to brew their own beer. This was when most beer was made that way, and beer was better for you than water. The malthouse with its furnace and the mill were together beside Abbey Creek, somewhere between West Ham and Stratford, where there have always been mills. It's mostly a sewage farm there now.

The maltster had a wife and a little daughter, and then the wife took a fever from the marshes by the creek, and there was only the little daughter.

Still, they managed, the maltster turning the malt and grinding it, and the girl sitting by the mouth of the furnace to keep it burning right.

"Not too hot, not too low," she would say, as she had heard her mother say, when she put coals on the fire, and in the warm place by the fire she often thought she heard the very words come to her again, even when she had not spoken out loud.

"It is my mother watching me," she said to herself; and, well, her father saw no tears because the furnace dried them up. And if it did not, then with the band that kept her hair back across her brow and caught the hot sweat, she could dry them for herself.

"Just wrap up well before you come from the fire," he said. "It was the cold of the creek that made your mother poorly."

So they got on together through the year, and then it was coming to the time of the Carnival and a busy time for brewers, and they worked day and night.

And sometimes the girl was left all alone and could not hear her father above raking the malt or feeding the wheel; so she wondered at that.

But the truth is, he was out courting. And if he didn't fill all his orders for malt that year, he filled his order for a new wife.

"You shall like her," he told his daughter. "And you shall have two big sisters, and they will take turn and turn about with your toil, and that will ease you."

"I am happy for you, Father," she said. And she thought she heard herself say, "Not too hot, not too low," down and dry before the fire. But, she thought, it was not her voice, and not her mother's.

There came a wedding, and she met her stepmother and her new sisters. They were very finely dressed for the occasion, she thought, and herself quite neat but not more than fancy.

"We shall be nice to her," said the tall sister.

"It is our nature to be kind," said the plump one.

"What a plain little thing," said the new mother. "We can be as nice as we like, but it won't make any difference."

The girl thought that in a very little time the two sisters would put away their finery and come into the malthouse and take their share of work.

"I will show you how to do it," she said, beside the furnace fire. "Not too hot, not too low."

"My dear child," said the tall sister, "all this heat. No wonder your skin is dried and cracked."

"And the ashes," said the plump one. "No wonder your hair is filled with grit."

"We have much more delicate things to do," said the tall one.

"So you will have to go on as you were," said the plump one. "We don't do servants' work."

"You shall do that," said the tall sister.

"We shall call you Clinker," said the plump one.

And that was that. She tended the furnace and was called Clinker, and made sure her tears were dry before she came into the house. And even there she had to cook and wash the dishes and eat in the kitchen while her new sisters were ladylike in the parlour.

And they grew more and more unkind as time went by, and when they were not complaining that gentlemen had forgotten to beg their hands in marriage they were complaining that Clinker was spoiling the food and making them ashamed.

However, before the next Carnival came round, but while poor Clinker was day and night at the furnace and night and day in the kitchen too, the two sisters began to be more cheerful, though they did not help Clinker at all.

The tall one explained that at the Closing Ball the King of the Carney was bound to notice her elegant figure and was sure to ask for her hand in marriage.

The plump one was sure the King of the Carnival would see how well she danced, and dance with no one else the whole night through.

And Clinker, well, she wished that there were two Kings who would take one sister each; so she wished them well.

But no one thought to ask her about the Carney, and certainly not about the Closing Ball, though she had been promised that she should go when she was old enough. But her father now seemed to have forgotten her.

So on the night of the Ball she sat alone by the furnace, where it was warm.

"Not too hot, not too low," she said to herself.

It was as if her mother's voice had said the words. "What was my name?" she wondered, because by now she had been nothing but Clinker for a year. "Oh well, no Clinker at the Carney.

Then a sprouted grain of barley fell off the edge of the floor above, where it had all been spread to dry.

There it lay on the brick floor. And then another tumbled down and lay beside it. And then another, and another, until there were six of them.

But Clinker did not see them stand in two lines, as if they knew what to do. She had wept four tears of misery, and one by one they filled her eyes and fell to the floor.

Then she wiped her face with the cloth she held the poker with, and was ready to cry again.

"Not too hot, not too low," said a voice that was not hers, and not her mother's, and not known to her at all.

And there, opening the fire door from the other side, was a little man in a white coat, standing among the embers, and stepping out of them.

Clinker was ready with the poker at once, because she did not know what this thing was.

"I am the Kilnman," said the man in the white coat, "You have looked after me these last years, and it is no longer your turn."

"But I have nothing else to do," said Clinker. "And my father needs my help."

"He shall have help," said the Kilnman. "He shall have willing help. But now, you do not want to be here, so where would you rather be?"

"Oh, at the Closing Ball of the Carney," said Clinker. "But I should not tell my dreams. And I am plain, and ash is in my hair."

"But you shall smile," said the Kilnman. "And no face is plain that smiles and laughs."

And with that he gathered up the spilt grains of malted barley and threw them out of the firestead and into the yard outside.

When they touched the ground the grains turned into horses, and the sprouts into riders on their backs.

"I will bring the scuttle of coals," said the Kilnman, picking it up and taking it out. And when it was out it rocked three times and became a coach for the horses and riders to pull.

Then the Kilnman jumped up to drive the coach. "I am ready to go," he said. "Get into the coach."

"But I am in a dress black with coals and burnt and very old," said Clinker. "And I am sure I shall wake up."

"You are not asleep," said the Kilnman. "Fling the poker-cloth about your shoulders, and then see."

So Clinker flung the poker-cloth about her shoulders, and

it turned into a gown of white and gold, heavy as an eiderdown.

"And my hair," said Clinker.

"Shake your head," said the Kilnman; and when she did the diamond dust floated about her and settled on her once more so that she glittered.

"And my plain, plain, face," said Clinker.

"Well, for that," said the Kilnman, "if you think it so, then draw your hairband across your eyes."

And Clinker did that, and could see well enough.

"Then away to the Closing Ball," said the Kilnman. "Only, at midnight by Stratford Abbey clock, you must leave and be soonest back beside the furnace; or this will all have never been."

"They will not know me," said Clinker. "My two step-sisters."

"They will not," said the Kilnman. "Nor will others; but then you are so plain. you say."

"I am so plain," said Clinker, "and just the furnace girl."

Then coach, horses, riders, coachman, and Clinker were at the steps of Stratford Town Hall, where the Closing Ball was to run from dusk to dawn.

Clinker got out in white and gold, and all the people turned to look at her.

"It is my pretty dress," she thought. "I'm glad they cannot see my face."

When she went inside at once a handsome man came straight to her, putting aside the partner he was dancing with. It was Clinker's plump sister, and once again Clinker was glad she wore her hairband as a mask, because the plump sister at once complained to the tall one, and sat at the edge of the ballroom.

But the handsome man took Clinker and he danced with her. And when that music was over he danced with her again.

"But who are you?" he asked. "You wear this mask of gold, I cannot tell."

"But who are you?" she asked.

"Me," he said. "I am no one; but tonight I am the King of Carnival."

"So there are others you must dance with," said Clinker. "Not me alone."

"Yes, you alone," he said. "Tonight and every night."

And he would not let her go. Not only the tall sister and the plump one, but every lady from all surrounding boroughs stamped her foot in rage, and sulked, and rattled with her fan.

But the King of the Carney would only dance with Clinker, Clinker all the time.

Then the Abbey clock began to clear its throat, and to ding-a-dong. And Clinker wished to remember all that had been, and not to have it as if had never been at all. So she flung herself from the King's grasp and ran for the doorway.

"Not so hasty," said the King of the Carney. "Do not go so soon."

"Not so fast, young woman," said the plump sister, leaping up in a rage. "I will have your eyes out," and she scratched at Clinker's face.

"Hold hard," said the tall sister. "I am to know you again, miss," and she scratched too.

But all they got was the sweatband, tearing it away. Clinker put her hands across her face and ran. The coach was waiting, and just as the Abbey clock struck its midnight bell she closed the door.

At once they were in the maltster's yard. The horses were once again grains of barley; the coach was a scuttle of coals, the Kilnman was running to the fire, and Clinker stood in the cold in her plain rags, with ashes in her hair.

"It was a dream," she said. "But I have it to remember always."

"Always," said the Kilnman. "Not too hot, not too low, but always with you."

The next day the two sisters were very bad-tempered. Clinker could do nothing right for them, and they would tell her nothing about the ball. And of course they did not ask her about it, because they knew she had been sitting beside the furnace while they danced. Though they had sat against the wall nearly all the time.

"He left halfway through," they told their mother and the stepfather. "At midnight the King of the Carney went away. And before that he had danced with a girl so old and ugly that she wore a mask all the time."

"Well there," said their mother, "at least no one here saw how you were so put out."

But a day or two later there was a letter from the town hall, sent out to all the girls who had been invited to the Closing Ball. It was from the King of the Carnival, and said not only that he had some property to restore, but that the true owner was to be his wife.

The two sisters thought about that.

"It is the mask," said the tall one.

"It would fit me," said the plump one.

"Ha," said the tall one. "You try first, then, and see what happens."

Then the king came, and it was indeed the mask he brought with him. But Clinker heard nothing of this, because she was out by the furnace, feeling very plain, but with happy memories.

The plump sister tried the mask first. It would not go on. "It is the cold weather," she said. "It makes my ears just a little larger."

"Nonsense," said the tall sister.

"Just wait a minute," said the plump one. She went into the kitchen and she cut off her ears. They bled horrid. But the mask would go on.

"But," said the King of the Carney, "I see it makes you unhappy."

"It is all so sudden," said the plump sister, and fell down in a faint and had to be taken to the hospital for stitches and bandages.

"It is me, of course," said the tall sister. But for her the problem was a little different. She said she had a cold, and went to the kitchen and cut off her nose. It ran ugly.

"I see it is still too tight," said the King.

"It is very comfortable," said the tall sister. But then the

cat had got up on the table and began carrying the nose
about, and the stepmother had to get it away and stitch her
daughter together.

"I am well out of the noise," said King. "That's it for this
house, is it?"

"That's it," said the stepmother.

So the King stepped out into the yard to rinse the blood
from the mask in the water butt.

Just at that time Clinker was fetching more coals for the
furnace.

"Who are you?" said the King of the Carney.

"But who are you?" she asked, though she very well
knew, and only wondered what she had done wrong for the
king to come after her, and so much blood on his hands,
fearing she had caused him to do some terrible deed.

Then she stood a moment, in the cold air, and flung the
poker-cloth about her shoulders, and seemed to stand in
white and gold.

And in a moment the King of the Carney found that the
mask fitted perfectly.

And, well, that night the barley malt burnt itself black
because there was no one to tend the furnace; and then the
two sisters were a long time learning the trade of not too
hot, not too low, but they wanted to do nothing else, being
now made so frightful by cutting themselves that they dared
not appear on any street.

They'd be at it yet, if it wasn't for canned beer made in the
big breweries.

∞ *The Dead Fairy* ∞

W here the Chicksand Estate is now, in Tower Hamlets, there were once fields growing salads and roots for the City markets, and people living in cottages right out in the country.

A young woman called Vanessa Cardew lived in one of the cottages, and in her fields she grew coles, which is cabbage, and beet. And while neighbouring farmers would ask her whether she would walk the church aisle with them, she would always say no.

"I'm just as well off with me alone," she said. "And what I haven't got I can fancy at no cost, there's nought else to do when I am hoeing beet or cutting coles."

So in time she got left behind in that way, and of course she wondered whether she was missing conversation; but she told herself that men were all kiss until they'd earned a fireside to sit by, and then they were all go and very likely gone.

But one day a little oldish, youngish, kind of fellow came by her door and wondered whether she had a cup of milk for him, because he was so weary of waiting. His name was Robin.

"Waiting?" said Vanessa Cardew. "What is Robin waiting for?"

"Oh," said he, "to be buried. It could happen any day, but it hasn't yet."

"I understand that," said Vanessa. "But you are no different from the rest of us." But she gave him some milk and a cut off the loaf.

"The difference is that I am dead," said Robin. But he drank at the milk like a live one. "I am only waiting to be buried."

Well, he's truthful, said Vanessa to herself. If it's true, mind.

"And now I'm a good worker," he said. "And I could hoe in among the beets in return for your kindness."

So Robin hoed in among the beets, row on row. And that night he slept out with the cow. The next day he said he hadn't yet earned his night's rest, and was cutting coles all day.

That night he laid by the house fire. And the next morning he carried beets and coles to market with Vanessa, and then wheeled her home on the cart.

The next day he laid the hedge on the north side; and the day after on the south; and so along.

"I've changed my mind," said Vanessa. "If you'll have me, Robin, you can thatch the cottage and paint the fence, and fill the kettle, while I go to fetch the parson."

"I'd not want to be buried so soon," said Robin. "Though I don't know when the time will come."

"The parson is for

the wedding only," said Vanessa. "I think we'll get along like that, day by day."

"Very well," said Robin. "But no church bells."

"It'll just be quiet," said Vanessa.

And so it was. The next day Robin took her up the aisle, and the parson said the words, and that was that, man and wife.

Or not, as the case might be.

"We'll hasten home," said Robin. "Churches are cold places to me, though I truly like the windows."

But they had not got out of the church before another wedding came to be done; and they had not got to the churchyard gate before that wedding was over too, and then the bells began to ring for it, just as the people liked.

"All should be well," said Robin. "But we should be out of the churchyard by now, so still hasten, Vanessa."

However, before Vanessa could reply, two of the bells struck at the same moment, with a great clash of sound.

"That is called firing," said Robin. And all at once, following the sound, or in the middle of it, there was silence, and the world stood still for Vanessa.

"Why, what is it?" she asked.

"When the bells fire God goes away," said Robin. "It is the only time a fairy can be buried, if he is caught in the churchyard, which is why I have been long dead."

"Come away," said Vanessa. "I will not bury you. You are my husband." But she could not move.

"You will remember me," he said. "I will send for you."

Then she saw crowds of fairies come pouring into the churchyard, bringing a coffin of willow bark, and a burying beetle, and pall-carriers.

They strapped Robin into the coffin (because fairies do not use nails), and carried him away, singing their strange songs, but whether it was glad or sorry singing Vanessa could not tell.

And there on the north side of the church they buried him, and went away like dust.

Vanessa was left there alone, with the bells still ringing. She made her way home alone, and sorely missed her fairy man. But she did not weep, because she could fancy worse things without being frightened.

"He has left me nothing but the hedges laid and the fences painted and the thatch tidied," she said. "I will be glad of that." But her fancies were drier from that day for the rest of the year.

But when that time was up she did what fairy wives will do. She laid an egg.

She put it in a nest of hay and kept it warm. She turned it, and she washed it, and it was no trouble. She was not a fairy wife, so she did not know what else to do.

Then one morning she found the egg cracked down the side, and the day after it was opening at the top, and on the evening of that day the shell was empty and out had come the baby thing.

"Now," said Vanessa, "if that had been on a cole I would have squashed it." Because it was a caterpillar, and it had eaten all the hay and begun on the shell of its egg.

"But this," said Vanessa, "is my own child, green as it is, and with two rows of legs as it has, and such a mouth."

She tried it on milk, but it would have none of that. She tried it on bread, but it spat that out. She tried it on apple, but it would not eat. She tried it on a cup of tea, but it just cried.

It took a leaf of cole and ate it all away, and that was its dinner that day.

In the morning it had grown fur. It was looking for more to eat. It would neither touch cheese nor try biscuit; but it was well away with another leaf of cole, and yet another still.

Vanessa put a collar on it and walked it in her little fields. On that first day it would eat a whole cole, stalk and all.

That night it slept on a stool. The next night it slept along the hearth. The night after that it pushed out the cow and slept there.

"What is it?" asked her neighbours.

"Children come in all shapes and sizes," said Vanessa. "This is as beautiful as any, and when the time comes he shall go to school."

But before that the time came when all the coles were finished.

And then all the beet were grazed to the ground.

After that the hedges went, and the caterpillar was so big the cow left home.

"He'll be better when he has his A B C," said Vanessa.

Last of all it ate the thatch, but left the chimney.

"Children eat you out of house and home," said Vanessa. "But they look after you in your old age."

When the thatch had gone the caterpillar stopped eating. He became tired and unloving, and would not go for a walk with Vanessa.

"What have I done wrong to him?" she wondered.

He went in among her apple treees. He had long since eaten every leaf, but the empty trees still stood. He climbed up one and along another, made himself a bed, got in it, pulled up the covers, and took no notice of anyone. But somewhere inside he was breathing and moving, so he was not dead.

"It is what the dormice do," said Vanessa.

Then it was winter, and all the fields were covered in snow. Vanessa had no roof and sat cold beside her fire.

She thought she might die, not being used to it like a dormouse.

But she lived through to the spring, thin as a rail. But the coles and beet were not growing again.

"I was never rich," she told a neighbour. "But I have had my fancies. Ah well." She thought she must now die, with nothing to take with her, and nothing to leave behind.

But her fancy did not come near what happened.

The caterpillar woke up in the sunshine. One morning Vanessa came out and found his bed split open, and him standing beside it.

"You have slept bad," she said, because he was black and wrinkled, and seemed not happy.

But it stretched out a leg and wiped an eye.

"It is a dragon," said the neighbours. "Fetch the soldiers."

"I know what that is," said Vanessa, and she fetched a dish of honey. The black thing put out a black tongue and licked up the honey.

Then it spread a wing. One side was mottled below and the other painted bright as a window in the church.

It spread the other wing, and moved them both.

"It is a butterfly," said the neighbours. "But too big to be proper."

Vanessa knew it was more than that. It was the child of the fairy husband called Robin, and it had been sent for her, as Robin promised. It waited for her now, and she climbed upon its back, and it flew away with her.

All the neighbours shook their heads, and when they told the parson he shook his head too and told them that liars went to perdition.

But where Vanessa went was more than her fancy ever told her; and where that is my fancy has not told me. But until the Chicksand Estate in Tower Hamlets was built there was a little thatchless cottage among the fields of coles, and I daresay it was Vanessa's.

The Bells of London Town

Gay go up, and gay go down,
   To ring the bells of London Town.
Bulls' eyes and targets,
   Say the bells of Saint Margaret's.
Brickbats and tiles,
   Say the bells of Saint Giles.
Oranges and lemons,
   Say the bells of Saint Clement's.
Pancakes and fritters,
   Say the bells of Saint Peter's.
Two sticks and an apple,
   Say the bells of Whitechapel.
Pokers and tongs,
   Say the bells at Saint John's.
Kettles and pans,
   Say the bells at Saint Anne's.
Maids in white aprons,
   Say the bells at Saint Catherine's
Old Father Baldpate,
   Say the slow bells at Aldgate.
You owe me five farthings,
   Say the bells of Saint Martin's.
You owe me ten shillings,

Say the bells of Saint Helen's.
When will you pay me?
Say the bells at Old Bailey.
When I grow rich,
Say the bells at Shoreditch.
Pray, when will that be?
Say the bells at Stepney.
I'm sure I don't know,
Says the great bell at Bow.
Here comes a candle to light you to bed
And here comes a chopper to chop off your head.